"Don't leave me

Every muscle that ha[...]
action hardened. Jon[...]
She wasn't crying, but the way her beautiful dark
eyes reached out to him let him know that she was
close.

"Please, stay with me."

It was in that moment that he knew there was no
other place he wanted to be.

"It'll be okay," he said. "I promise."

Sirens could be heard in the distance. The crying
and yelling still sounded around them. For the first
time since the car had nearly run them down, he
realized the silver case hadn't left Kate's side.

She'd kept it with her through it all.

What was in it?

And why was it worth killing for?

BE ON THE LOOKOUT: BODYGUARD

———

TYLER ANNE SNELL

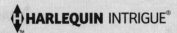

HARLEQUIN INTRIGUE®

This book is for Virginia Spears.

You're a beautiful, brilliant, hilarious sunflower. I hope we grow old
together and can still make fun of all the silly things we did when we were
younger. You're one of the best humans I know and, for that, you deserve
much more than a dedication in a book. However, that's all I'm working
with for now, so I hope this will do, you exotic, sparkling unicorn, you.

ISBN-13: 978-0-373-69925-4

Be on the Lookout: Bodyguard

Copyright © 2016 by Tyler Anne Snell

Recycling programs
for this product may
not exist in your area.

Printed in U.S.A.

Tyler Anne Snell genuinely loves all genres of the written word. However, she's realized that she loves books filled with sexual tension and mysteries a little more than the rest. Her stories have a good dose of both. Tyler lives in Florida with her same-named husband and their mini "lions." When she isn't reading or writing, she's playing video games and working on her blog, *Almost There*. To follow her shenanigans, visit tylerannesnell.com.

Books by Tyler Anne Snell

Harlequin Intrigue

Orion Security

Private Bodyguard
Full Force Fatherhood
Be on the Lookout: Bodyguard

Manhunt

CAST OF CHARACTERS

Jonathan Carmichael—As one of the original Orion Security Group agents, seeing his friends settling down makes this bodyguard yearn for a change. So when he takes on one last client, he's not prepared for the beautiful brunette with dangerous secrets. When it's clear someone wants to end any chance of her having a future, can this bodyguard abandon his dreams of putting down roots to make sure she survives the present?

Kate Spears—Nearly consumed with her research, this young scientist believes that her trip to New York City will change everything. However, when threats start to surround her and the bodyguard she didn't want around, she starts to see that danger does indeed follow her every step. Can she look past years of near self-isolation to the man ready to sacrifice everything to keep her safe?

Greg Calhoun—An old family friend, this man of science has helped guide Kate throughout the years and doesn't stop when things become dangerous.

Jake Harper—Kate's childhood friend is as mysterious as the scientist's work but makes it clear he'll do anything to help out the bodyguard and his friend.

Lola Teague—Manager of a New York City hotel, this woman is all business when her guests' lives are put in danger.

Mark Tranton—Jonathan's closest friend and fellow Orion agent, this bodyguard's continuing happiness helps show Jonathan he wants more from life.

Nikki Waters—Founder of Orion Security Group and one of Jonathan's closest friends, this boss is more than willing to give Jonathan what he wants, just not before he takes on one last client.

Chapter One

He wouldn't tell anyone this, but the fight almost ended much differently.

The punch that landed squarely against his jaw almost knocked him out. Pain, bright and bold, exploded along the bone as the blow connected. It made him stagger to the side, and for a moment he struggled with fighting the urge to cradle the pain and seek refuge.

Or pass out. Blackness fringed the edges of his vision.

But Jonathan Carmichael wasn't that easy to take down.

He dropped low into a crouch and swung his leg around. His attacker wasn't fast enough to move out of the way. His legs were swept out from under him and he hit the ground hard. The wheeze of someone who had lost their breath escaped from his lips.

Jonathan wasn't where he needed to be physically—the punch really had done a number on him—but he knew the hired thug wasn't just going to lie down and take it. Plus, he still had someone to protect.

Out of his periphery, Jonathan saw the door behind him and to the left was still closed. Fleetingly, he wondered if Martin actually locked the door like he had been told.

"You—gonna—gonna pay," the thug started to wheeze out, but Jonathan didn't have time for a speech. He turned on his heel and leveled the man with his own knockout punch. The muscle-clad baddie didn't wage an internal war of whether or not he was going to slip into unconsciousness. Or, if he did, he didn't win the battle.

His head clunked against the hardwood while the rest of his body relaxed.

"I'm *gonna* have a tall beer tonight," Jonathan said, tenderly touching his chin. He winced. "That's what I'm gonna do, all right."

He nudged the guy's foot with his work boot before feeling comfortable enough to walk back to the door his client was behind. Trying the doorknob, he cursed beneath his breath.

"Martin, I told you to lock this."

His client, an older man who was five feet three inches of scatterbrain, didn't offer an apology for not listening to his bodyguard. Instead his eyes widened at Jonathan's appearance.

"You're bleeding," Martin exclaimed. He pointed to his eyebrow and then his lip.

"Don't worry," he hedged, temporarily forgetting he had other injuries. "It's the jaw that hurts the worst."

"And the bad man?" Martin didn't try to see out

into the other room. To him the hired gun was his own personal hell. An evil man who had threatened him, stalked him and attacked him. All in an attempt to exact revenge for sending his boss to prison. Jonathan remembered when the man had come into Orion Security Group's front doors begging for protection, for a bodyguard to keep him safe. The police hadn't believed he was being targeted, but Jonathan's boss had.

A call Jonathan was grateful for and so was Martin.

"He won't hurt you anymore."

Martin's entire body sagged in relief.

"Thank you, son. Thank you."

Jonathan nodded, ignoring how the endearment struck a sore chord. Before he could stop it, the invisible wall that he had built for thirty-three years sprang up. He cleared his throat.

"Tell me you at least called nine-one-one," he deadpanned. Martin's eyes widened again, guilt written clearly across his face.

Jonathan let out a long breath.

"Call them while I go tie up our friend," he ordered, pulling the zip ties from one of his cargo pants' pockets. Martin nodded and for once listened.

The thug, a man around the same age as Jonathan but who had obviously had a much harder life, stayed unconscious while Jonathan tied his wrists together in front of his stomach. Just to be safe, he patted him down, revealing a wicked pocketknife and a wad of cash. There was no ID, but Jonathan didn't need it.

He felt as if he knew the man on some level. Fiercely loyal to his boss.

Hardened by life from the streets with scars that bore testament to that theory.

Determination unwavering.

Was he that different?

Would this have been Jonathan's life had he not run into his current boss all those years ago?

Jonathan shook his head. He'd learned at a young age that *what-ifs* did more harm than they ever did good.

"I called them—they're on their way and a little confused," Martin said from the doorway, eyes staying away from the man who had tormented him for months. "But then this man called?" He held Jonathan's phone away from him with a shrug.

The bodyguard quickly took the phone, confused, as well.

"Carmichael here."

"Why does the client have your phone?"

Jonathan cut a grin as the voice of one of Orion's finest—and his closest friend—filled his ear.

"Well, look who it is! Mark Tranton, back from vacation."

A chuckle came through the airwaves.

"Well, you couldn't expect me to pass on a free weeklong stay at a beachside bungalow, could you?" Mark exclaimed.

"The old Mark would have," Jonathan reminded his

friend. "But the new Mark is a lot more fun, so I guess it's understandable."

"The new Mark also has two ladies who would never let him pass on a former client's generosity like that," the other man added with another laugh. Jonathan had known Mark for almost a decade and was glad to see his friend happy with his girlfriend and her young daughter. "Now, why did the client answer your phone?"

Jonathan gave his fellow bodyguard a rundown of the exchange from the moment the man picked the front door lock to the knockout minutes before Mark called. He could hear the concern in Mark's voice as he questioned Jonathan's injuries, but Jonathan's walls were still up. He brushed the concerns off.

"The cops should be here soon, so I need to go," he started. "Wait, did you need something?"

"Yeah, but it can wait. Give me a call when you land in Dallas and I'll meet you at Orion."

Jonathan agreed to that and they ended the call.

The bodyguard slid his phone back into his pocket and took another long look at the man on the ground.

I could have been you.

TWO DAYS LATER Jonathan was cruising through Dallas, Texas, in the familiar comfort of his old, worn Range Rover. It was raining, but not enough to spoil his homecoming or Mark's insistence that he come straight to Orion's office. He wondered what all the fuss was about but didn't think on it too much as he puttered his way through afternoon traffic.

Before Orion he'd been an agent with Redstone Solutions, an elite and very private security agency. With more funding than they knew what to do with—and very little care for those who couldn't afford basic safety—he'd had contracts that had taken him all over the world. Orion, operating on a smaller financial but higher moral scale, still made him travel the nation. Through all of his travels, though, he could safely come to one concrete conclusion: traffic anywhere was horribly annoying.

There were some things he missed about his hometown, but this wasn't one of them.

The rain let up by the time he reached the one-story building with its Orion Security Group sign blaring atop the front doors. Steam rose from the parking lot asphalt as he stretched. Unlike Mark or even Oliver, another close friend and Orion employee, Jonathan had a wide wingspan and stood taller than the two at six-three. Growing up, his long limbs had made him self-conscious—catching names like "String Bean" and "Stretch"—but being a bodyguard had taught him how to use his lean body to his advantage.

Strength and speed were two traits he trained hard to keep.

Orion's lobby had long windows tinted to keep the Texas sun at bay. It kept the lobby cool as Jonathan passed by the desk where their cyber-techy secretary, a young woman named Jillian, sat. At her absence, he felt a sort of alertness flare. Just because she wasn't in the lobby didn't mean he should think something ominous was going on.

Yet, as he walked through the door and down the hallway that led to the common area for employees, Jonathan couldn't shake the growing feeling of unease. Especially since he had passed empty offices belonging to Mark and Thomas, another Orion agent.

"Hello?" he said, rounding the corner to the grazing area, as he liked to call the open-area lounge for employees between the boss's office and the training room. Normally it was a comfortable space to relax or play a way-too-competitive game of Ping-Pong, never too much action going on. So when he found it filled with people who yelled, "Surprise," when he was in view, while a brightly colored banner that said Congratulations hung above him, Jonathan was wholly taken aback.

His eyes roamed over the many people bunched together. Among them he found Mark, his boss, in-house Orion employees and a few people he'd never met. He was sure he looked like a jackass standing there gaping.

"I don't understand?" he asked when the cheers had died down.

An attractive woman with short, dark red hair laughed. She was Nikki Waters, founder and main boss at Orion, as well as one of his three closest friends.

"To be honest, this—" she motioned to the banner and then to the people next to her "—isn't really for you, but we couldn't resist trying to surprise you.

Though, I guess it could count if we said, 'Congrat-ulations for a supremely well-done job of handling yourself this week!'" She held up a champagne flute—something he realized the other partygoers also held—and lifted it in the air. "To Jonathan Carmichael for an excellent job well-done!"

A chorus of "hear, hear" sounded.

"Thanks," he said, still uncertain. "But who is this all really for?"

Nikki looked at Mark, who stepped to the side. Kelli, Mark's girlfriend, showed herself.

"Us," she answered before holding up her left hand. A ring graced her finger, but it was the smile on Mark's face that really sold it.

"You're kidding me," Jonathan exclaimed, a smile as pure as they came pulling up the corners of his lips. "You two are getting hitched?"

They laughed in unison.

"You better believe it, best man!"

Jonathan's happiness for his best friend pushed him forward and he gave the many-muscled man a big hug. Mark, knowing Jonathan wasn't big on shows of affec-tion, knew not to comment. Instead he returned it be-fore passing the second embrace on to his future wife. The rest of the party went back to their own mingling as Jonathan took a step back to congratulate the two of them again.

"I wanted to wait to tell everyone after I'd told you, but this one here got a little too chatty." Mark looked at Kelli, who just laughed. A woman Jonathan didn't recognize pulled Nikki's and her attention away, leaving Mark and Jonathan alone.

"So should we talk about your face?" the bodyguard asked. Jonathan knew how it looked—a cut above his right lip, a bandage on his eyebrow and a gnarly bruise across his jawline—but he was happy that no one else had brought it up while he was in front of everyone.

"Don't worry, it feels worse than it looks," he joked. "So, best man, really?" Jonathan didn't want to keep talking about his previous job when he'd just been extended an honor that could be taken as the epitome of male friendship. Mark clapped him on the shoulder.

"Who else would I pick? Now go put your stuff away and we'll talk bachelor party ideas." Mark wiggled his eyebrows. Once again it reminded Jonathan of how much happier his friend had become in the past year of being with Kelli and her daughter. Life, according to him, had become more enjoyable than even he had imagined.

A mixture of longing, sadness and regret exploded in Jonathan's chest as he set his pack down behind his desk. From the open door he could see Kelli take Mark's hand even though the two were in separate conversations.

Looking back Jonathan would realize that it was in that moment that he made his next decision, but while he was still in the moment he would think it was when Nikki walked into the room to give him a new client file.

"I don't want to be a field agent anymore," he responded, surprising the two of them. "I'm missing out on life, Nikki, and I don't want to anymore." She took a seat. Jonathan continued, "Mark's getting married and already has a little family. Oliver has a kid on the way. I—" He struggled to find the words.

"Want to grow roots," she supplied.

"Yes, but I can't do that if I'm never in one spot for long."

"So you want a desk job," she added.

He nodded.

Nikki Waters wasn't an easy woman to ruffle. She pursed her lips but didn't try to sway his decision.

"Okay," she said instead.

"Okay?" He'd half expected her to be angry. Other than Mark he was the highest-ranking field agent.

"When I started Orion, I knew it would be a lot of work, and you've been an integral part in helping me carry that workload. That's included sacrificing your personal life, I've noticed. If you want to stay in one place, we can make that happen."

"So…that's it?"

Nikki held up her index finger.

"Now, I didn't say *that*."

Chapter Two

Kate Spears sighed as she looked down at the letter covered in blood. It, like the handful of others before it, was folded and had been placed squarely on the middle of her doormat.

Her father, Deacon, a man who was made of worry more than anything else, was lagging behind her, talking on his phone. His current worry that his wife, her stepmother, was having a less than good day at work rated low on the stress totem pole. But like his ability to worry, he took pride in being a good husband. So there he paced across the sidewalk next to Kate's mailbox, listening to his wife's woes as his daughter tried to figure out how to handle the bloody stationery.

"If this isn't a true case of the Mondays, I don't know what is," she muttered as she riffled through her larger-than-life purse. Unable to distinguish or adhere to the line between work and home, she found the pack of latex gloves within seconds and pulled one on. In another pocket of her purse she found a clean baggie. Being a scientist had its perks.

"Okay, honey, love you, too," Deacon said, suddenly closer. Kate panicked and stuffed the note into the plastic bag along with her latex glove as quickly as she could. The bag was then stuffed into the purse. All within seconds. It made Kate momentarily feel like she'd gotten away with something. Though, in hindsight, she would realize there were few things you could get past Deacon Spears. "Are we going to pretend that I didn't just see you shove several things into your purse?"

Kate let out another long breath. While she didn't always leave work at work, she didn't want to bring this conversation home. Especially not during lunch with her father.

"I don't know what you mean," she lied, finally opening the front door.

"And there's the higher pitch to your voice," he pressed, following her into the entryway of her town house. Normally she would place her purse beneath the table next to the front door, but she kept it close to her side this time. Or else her father would already be going through it.

"Can you stop analyzing me? I'm not data, you know," she said, grinning. While Deacon owned a hardware store, Kate still insisted on cheesy jokes from her field of work. He usually laughed at them. Not now. The fake mirth didn't dissuade Deacon's determination. He crossed his arms over his chest and used the voice reserved only to scold his daughter. Never mind that she was twenty-nine, had a mortgage and had just completed a five-year project that could save countless lives.

"Kathryn Gaye Spears, I don't know why you're lying to me, but I do know you better cut the crap now."

Kate physically shied away from the accusation by moving down the hallway and into the kitchen. Her hand clung to the strap of her purse as if the contact would somehow help it magically know it needed to hide until lunch was over.

"Dad, do you want some coffee?" she hedged. "I *really* need some." Deacon followed silently and stood like a statue next to the refrigerator. From growing up with him, Kate knew it was a matter of minutes before his steely resolve broke hers, but Kate was also stubborn. She met her father's blue-eyed stare with her own brown-eyed one and was reminded in full how the two of them looked nothing alike.

Short yet solid, Deacon had been blessed with a hereditary tan from his half-Hispanic mother, but had his father's once blond-white hair—even though it was sparse at the crown around an almost shiny bald spot. Besides his overall look that just cried "retiring in Florida," the fifty-six-year-old had a young, slightly rounded face. One that was partially hidden by another sun-bleached mustache he said his wife Donna thought made him look regal.

Kate, on the other hand, was the spitting image of her mother. Before her death, Cassandra Spears had been taller than her husband when she wore high heels—though she never did—and much leaner. In the same respect that was true for Kate. At five-nine, she could see over Deacon's head with heels—though she also wasn't a fan—and was lean but without the muscles that had been a necessary part of Cassandra's job in law enforcement. Kate also shared the rich brown hair her mother had once sported, waving to her shoulders with thick bangs across her forehead, and her mother's teardrop face and full lips. The only way she differed from either parent was the less than active tan that graced her skin. In the last five years Kate had resided in labs or over her computer screen during almost all waking hours. There was no time to go outside and play in the sun for her.

Though, as her father's stare bored holes into her own, Kate thought a break for the park might be better than what was about to happen.

"It's really not that big of a deal," Kate finally conceded. "Can't you just let me deal with it?"

Her father shook his head with a firm no.

Defeated, she put her purse on the counter and pulled out the baggie and its contents.

Alarmed wasn't a strong enough word for Deacon's reaction.

"Is that blood?" he asked, voice a mile past concerned. Careful not to rumple the letter inside, he took the bag and set it on the counter.

"It's made to look like it, but if it's like the last one it's synthetic." His eyes widened.

"The last one? You mean you've gotten one before this?"

Kate gave one more sigh. She'd hoped to avoid this conversation with her father until after her trip, when she was sure the letters would stop altogether. Sitting on one of the bar stools opposite him, she explained.

"Over the last few months I've received a handful of letters here and at the office," she admitted. "Only this one and the last one were covered in what *looks* like human blood, but we tested and confirmed it to be fake. Though, I still wouldn't touch that without gloves on." She pulled another set out of her purse and passed them to her father—a man curious enough to want to pull the letter out. Silently he slipped them on and did just that. Kate quickly put down a paper towel so the blood—fake or not—wouldn't touch the granite.

"It's covered front and back with writing," he observed, squinting at the handwritten letters. It was identical to all of the other notes she'd received. "But it's only one word, repeated. *Zastavit.*" He kept saying the word, as if tasting it to figure out its root.

"I think it's Czech," she said after a moment.

"Are you sure?"

She shrugged. "No, but I can guarantee it means 'stop.'"

His eyebrows rose in question.

She held up her index finger and made a quick trip to her bedroom. There she picked up a small box and brought it back to her father. Sitting back down, she waited for him to open it and extract the bundle of letters.

"Only a handful of letters? How many hands are you talking about in this scenario?" The letters numbered eighteen in total. Each had a single word repeated over the paper's entirety.

"They are all in different languages, but they all roughly translate to the word *stop*," she explained. "Plus, the first one was in English. I suppose to help me out just in case I didn't understand…or, you know, use a translator or the internet."

"Stop…stop what?" Realization lit his features before Kate had time to answer. "Your research."

She shrugged. "I suppose so. That's the only thing I really have going on in my life. Unless they want me to stop drinking coffee. Which, I'll be frank, isn't going to happen anytime soon."

"Dammit, Kate!" Her father slammed his free hand down on the counter, making her jump. "Stop joking about this!" He waved the note closest to him— the Hungarian one—in the air. "These are *threats*, not some love letters. Someone obviously invested a lot of thought and time into these."

"But they aren't threats, Dad," she insisted. "They are simply eclectic suggestions. No threat of harm has been given in any of them."

"But they've been delivered to your *home*, Kate!"

"And that's what I told the cops after the second one I received."

He was surprised at that.

"What did they say?"

"Exactly what I just said. They aren't really threats and nothing else has happened. They suggested putting a camera on the front porch, but…" She quieted.

"But what?"

"But I've been so busy preparing for the convention that I keep forgetting." Her father seemed to be trying very hard to keep his anger at his daughter's apparent lack of concern under control. He placed the letters back in the box and the newest one back into its bag. He slid that one over when done.

"You will test this as soon as possible to make sure it is in fact fake. I am calling in to the store and taking off the rest of the day. Make me that coffee you mentioned." He picked the box up and walked to the eat-in table. "I'm going to look through all of these in silence while I try to figure out what I did to deserve such a stressful child."

KATE PINCHED THE bridge of her nose and hoped the pain behind her dark brown eyes was a tease and not the beginnings of a headache. Sprawled out on her bed, amid her suitcase and carry-on, she called upon every entity there was and begged that the headache would stay far, far away.

She didn't need any more complications than she was already dealing with.

"Having a bodyguard is not that big a deal," her father said from the doorway. Since learning about the notes a week ago, she'd had constant supervision and parental advice. "Stop being such a baby!"

Kate, often referred to as brilliant by her supervisor, stuck out her tongue before responding.

"I'm not being a baby," she retorted, trying to keep

the whine from her voice. "I think I'm reacting normally given the circumstances."

"Most daughters would be grateful, you know."

She laughed.

"Most daughters don't have their fathers go behind their backs and hire *bodyguards* to supervise their trips to life-changing work functions!"

He managed to look momentarily guilty before shooting back with a response. "Well, most daughters don't—" He held up his hand, stopping himself. "Listen, we can sit here and fight about this all day while you lie next to your empty luggage, or you can just take the gesture with graciousness and understand that I only have one baby girl and that's you." His voice took on an edge that Kate recognized as vulnerability from the almost always strong man. It killed the less-than-nice reply she'd had waiting on the tip of her tongue. He walked over and took a seat next to her. She sat up to look him in the eyes.

"It's because of that fact that I can say this without getting into trouble," he started. Kate swallowed, unsure whether or not she was about to get into more trouble. However, when he continued, his voice was kind. "You've spent most of your life fighting to help people you'll never meet by doing research and working tirelessly in labs. Along the way you've achieved a level of greatness I never could have, and for that I'll be forever proud… But your drive—your dedication— often puts blinders up, making it hard for you to see the big picture. While your research is important, *you* are, too. You've tried to keep your work a secret, but what have I told you about secrets?"

"They don't exist."

He smiled.

"Someone will always tell someone else. It's the law of the land. And one that your mother tried to teach us. Someone obviously knows something, and whether or not it's the truth or some half-baked version of it, they have set their sights on you. Now, you've told me this convention will change everything. Well, I want to make sure you're there to see that through and continue to see it through long after it's over. Because even though you won't see the big picture—and its danger— I'll tell you right now that it's there." He patted her knee. "So, please, accept this protection, if only to give your old man some peace of mind."

Kate watched as a range of emotions played across her father's face. It reminded her of all the sacrifices he'd had to make to raise her on his own since she was nine. Never once asking anything of her.

Until now.

"Because I love you and can see your point, I'll make a deal with you," she offered. "I will humor you by accepting the protection of only *one* bodyguard. Any more than that will bring unwanted attention and, well, freak me out a little. So one and that's it, okay?"

He looked like he was ready to fight her again, but after a moment he nodded.

"Okay." He stuck out his hand to shake. "Deal."

They shook and she rolled her eyes. Their tender moment dissipated as he stood and stretched.

"Now, I have to ask, how exactly are you *paying* for this bodyguard service?" Like Kate, her father wasn't particularly wealthy. He worked at the hardware store he and his wife of five years owned.

"I was lucky enough to get connected to a place that works for free on cases they believe need it. One of my customers worked a news story for them when he lived in Dallas and was kind enough to give me a reference." He grinned.

"Oh, so they're amateurs, then."

"Definitely not. Their track record is impressive, to say the least," he answered. "Don't worry, I vetted them pretty well."

"So why exactly are they doing it for free?" she asked, perplexed. Deacon smiled wide.

"I guess that's a question you'll just have to ask your bodyguard."

Chapter Three

Traffic.

Here it was again.

Jonathan looked out his rental's window and snorted.

"Welcome to New York City," he said to himself.

He'd been stuck in standstill traffic for the last half hour thanks to a fender bender that had escalated to the point of the cops being called. It had made the two lanes of traffic that had been moving along nicely stop dead.

Unnecessary. Annoying. Unpleasant.

It probably didn't help that he could use all three descriptors for his current client, Kathryn Spears. Instead of waiting for him at the airport like Nikki and the woman's father had agreed on the night before, Jonathan had landed to a voice mail from her saying she'd gone ahead to the hotel.

Because, in her words, "I really need some better coffee."

After ten more minutes of waiting, traffic finally started to pick up again. Jonathan had spent the time while he waited going over the route to the hotel in an attempt to not get lost. He'd been to New York before and he knew the frustration of getting turned around this close to Times Square. Thankfully he avoided any misdirection, a feat considering if he had missed the turn into the hotel's parking garage—an almost hidden entrance due to the sidewalk that was barely sloped for a car to drive up—he would have had to take a series of left turns until he made his way back. Costing him more time away from fulfilling Orion's end of the contract.

He parked, sent a text to Nikki to let her know he'd finally gotten in and collected his bag. It contained a suit, pressed and folded, along with a myriad of pristine yet flexible clothing. It was light but had everything he needed for the Friday-through-Tuesday stay—not the longest contract he'd done nor the shortest. But, as he'd told Nikki, it would be his last. In his mind he went over the layout of the building as he rode up in the elevator. Above the parking garage, there were four floors. A lounge area branched off the lobby on the first floor with guests having access to a twenty-four-hour gym. There were two sets of stairs on opposite sides of the building with two elevators positioned next to them, diagonal from the lobby front desk. The front entrance led directly to the sidewalk that ran along the street.

Jonathan hadn't stayed at the dismal pink-painted hotel before, but Jillian had walked him through its layout before he'd left. It was nice to know what he was going into versus going in blind. Orion agents prided themselves on being prepared—though that wasn't always easy, considering people often did surprising things—and since Orion's expansion three years ago they'd gotten better at it. Even when a contract changed at the last second.

He looked at his reflection in the elevator door and let out a grunt. Not getting the best sleep the night before and catching an early flight, he hoped the client didn't notice the dark circles beneath his eyes. He blamed the chatty man who'd had the aisle seat next to him. It made him wonder if Kathryn was like that, recalling what he had been told initially by Nikki at Mark's engagement party.

"I wouldn't ask you to take this one, since, for one, you just got back, and, two, you just asked for a desk job. But the man requesting our services was so concerned...I could almost feel it myself." Nikki's eyes had traveled to the wall at that. It was a blank space, but he knew on the other side was her real target. A single picture of a young woman. The reason behind Orion's origin. The woman who had changed their lives, whom Nikki, Oliver, Mark and Jonathan couldn't have been what they were now without. The woman they hadn't saved. "He lives in Florida but heard about us through one of Thomas's recent clients. His daughter has been receiving some really troubling letters."

"His daughter?"

"Yes, a scientist—book smart but maybe not exactly up to par on the common sense. Her father, Deacon—what a name—says she's pretty nonchalant about the whole thing, but he's completely freaked. She's due to present her research at a convention in New York City on Sunday and he's worried the person or persons sending her the letters—to her home, I might add—might try to cause her harm before she can make it there."

"And that's where we come in."

"Hopefully that's where you come in."

Jonathan respected his boss and friend too much to turn the request down on the spot. Though he had been on the fence about it until the next day.

When she'd shown him the pictures of the letters Deacon had faxed over, they'd made a chill run up his spine despite his calm.

"Okay, I'm in."

And he'd stayed in even after the call had come in that said scientist refused to have more than one bodyguard around. Never mind her safety was in question.

The doors slid open and Jonathan made his way to check in with a suddenly sour mood hanging over his head at the thought of Kathryn Spears. Other than the basic information about her, he really didn't have much to go on, but he had already formed an opinion about her.

She was controlling, apathetic and had an ego. There were no doubts about it.

"Welcome, and how may I help you?" chirped the front desk attendant. He looked to be in his early twenties. His name tag read Jett.

Jonathan set down his bag and started to take out his ID.

"Check-in for Jonathan Carmichael." He passed his driver's license over as well as the company credit card, having done the hotel check-in dance many times before. Another part of this routine was his next question.

"Can you tell me if my friend has checked in yet? The name's Kathryn Spears."

The man looked back up and without missing a beat nodded.

"About an hour ago."

That surprised Jonathan.

"You remember her?" he asked.

"Yeah, the first thing she did was ask for coffee that was actually good." Jett didn't seem to be offended by the question. "I sent her to a café a block over." His eyes went over Jonathan's shoulder. "I guess she found some."

Jonathan didn't have to follow the man's gaze too far. Walking through the front doors, Kathryn had a cup between her hands and no trace of a smile across her lips. She met his stare with recognition he didn't expect and made a beeline for him.

"Mr. Carmichael," she said, stretching out her free hand. There was no question in the greeting. "Glad to see you finally made it."

Despite himself he grinned.

"Miss Spears, glad to see you were able to get that coffee that was so important." They shook and he was once again surprised by the woman. Not only was her grip firm, but she held it longer than necessary, squeezing tight as she answered.

"Two coffees, actually."

They dropped hands but his grin stayed. Even though he'd been shown her picture before he'd left Orion, the still of the woman sitting behind a desk covered in papers didn't do the woman before him justice. She was attractive, sure, but there was something else there that caught and held his attention. An unspoken element that he couldn't yet place or define.

Suddenly, Jonathan Carmichael was intrigued by his client.

"I would have waited for you," she continued, voice notably cool, "but I'll be honest, I think you being here is a bit unnecessary."

Jonathan let out a laugh at that, considering earlier he had thought the same about her.

"Don't you want to play it safe rather than be sorry?" he asked.

Kathryn's lip quirked up at the corner. Her smile wasn't humorous.

"I'd rather not have to worry about a bodyguard following me around everywhere, watching my every move while I get ready for one of the largest career moves of my life." She popped her hip out to the side a fraction, he noticed. "That would be my choice if I'd been given one."

Jonathan couldn't decide if the way she spoke was born out of ego or frustration, but he definitely felt a chill wafting from each word. Part of him instantly felt the need to defend his skills and the company that was more than just his employer but an important part of his life. However, Jett was obviously still listening in, so the bodyguard went a more judicious route.

"The Orion Security Group doesn't force clients to hire them," he pointed out. "It was your father who did that, and you consented. As for watching your every move while I'm on the job, I can assure you that—if I'm doing said job correctly—my eyes won't be on *you* but on your surroundings, trying to keep you safe. So if you have a problem with this arrangement, it's your father—and really, yourself—you'll need to be speaking with."

Kathryn didn't immediately respond. When she did it was clipped, definitely chilly.

"Noted. Now, if you'll excuse me, I need to do some work up in my room."

She started to turn to go—already testing the boundaries of his job as her bodyguard—when Jonathan smiled once again.

"Hey, I'll walk with you on the way to mine." She gave him a questioning look. "Oh, didn't your dad tell you? He requested we have adjoining rooms."

Jonathan might not have known the scientist long, but he knew he'd struck a nerve with that comment.

It was going to be an interesting few days.

KATE DIDN'T WANT to wait for the bodyguard. No matter how attractive he'd turned out to be. The picture she'd been forwarded from her father and Orion's Nikki Waters had shown her a lightly tanned man who looked like a stock image a website might use to show an everyman, not a bodyguard. He had seemed flat, one-dimensional. Someone who would easily blend into the background and, hopefully, not bother her.

However, in person she'd been surprised to see that maybe she'd misjudged him in that department. His dark blue eyes had depth, his facial features were sharp and his goatee was trimmed and neat, matching the jet-black hair that stood an inch or two high. He wore a gray tee and jeans and he wore them well. When he turned back to the desk attendant, she even spotted the bottom of a tattoo on the back of his upper arm, peeking out under his sleeve.

Maybe Jonathan Carmichael wasn't the type of man to blend.

"This is a massive invasion of privacy," Kate commented as she led them into the elevator. Like the hotel, it was dated. She pressed the second-floor button and hoped above all hopes that it didn't get stuck. Her nerves had been rubbed the wrong way, annoyed at her father and the man next to her. Getting trapped in the small space with him would most likely incite a flurry of rudeness from her. She was already having a hard time being polite without the added close proximity.

"Again, I'll remind you that your father hired Orion and you agreed," he said, not looking at her but obviously surveying the elevator. He was tall enough to reach up and push against the ceiling—trying to do what, she wasn't sure.

"I meant the adjoining-room situation," she corrected.

Jonathan stopped his inspection and gave her a dry smile.

"Just because there's a door there doesn't mean I'm going to use it. I don't even have a key. We just wanted the rooms to be close, and since it's an older hotel they just happen to share a door." His eyebrow rose. "Unless you want me to get *you* a key?"

Kate felt heat crawl up her neck.

"No," she said quickly. "I don't need or want one."

"Good. Then there shouldn't be a problem."

The elevator doors slid open and Kate hurried with her coffee to her room down the hall. Jonathan was right behind her with his bags.

"I'm going to look in your room, okay?" he said as she pulled out her key card. "I'd like to know the layout, just in case."

Kate wanted to argue, but was trying to channel her inner Spears' manners. She still rolled her eyes.

"Sure, why not?" She opened the door and swung it wide for the bodyguard. "Knock yourself out."

He moved past her, bags still in hand, into the room. For a moment she worried about her more intimate things being left out in the open, but it was a baseless fear. She was meticulous, a trait that had bled over from her professional life into her personal one. She'd already unpacked and sorted her things.

"To be honest, I expected something different," Jonathan said, apparently okay with his inspection.

"Something different?" she repeated. "Like a man in a mask lying in wait?"

The corner of his lips pulled up a fraction.

"I meant I expected to see, I don't know, test tubes and beakers on the nightstands. Aren't you a scientist?"

Kate walked over to the small desk in the corner and leaned against it. She felt a twitch try to pull her own lips into a small smile, but she tamped it down.

"Generally labeled, yes, I suppose." She took a sip of her coffee. "What else do you know about my work?"

If Jonathan knew about her project, she was sure she'd have seen some kind of reaction to her question. However, the man simply shrugged.

"If you're asking do I know what you're currently working on—why you're here for the convention—I don't. Orion tries to look into a client's life without being intrusive. Our analysts dip into your past and present to try to find potential threats, but we don't overstep. Your father and Nikki made it clear that, as far as your work goes, the only person who can tell me about it is you." He paused, tilting his head slightly. "And I suspect that that information is something you won't be sharing with me."

Before Kate could stop it, the image of a bloodied woman tied to a chair flashed across her vision. Head bent over, body beaten. Her last breath having already left her body hours before.

The image was something she'd had to confront for a long time. It twisted the very core of her heart.

"No," she said, voice turned to ice. "I won't."

Chapter Four

Jonathan wasn't invited to stay past the woman's answer. He didn't want to, either. Kathryn's voice had gone steely, her eyes almost to slits, and even from his spot across the room he'd been able to see her breathing change. Whatever she'd just experienced, it pulled his curiosity to the forefront, but he kept his mouth shut. What was behind her dark eyes was something darker. Something he had no business seeking out.

His room was to the right and was an exact replica of hers. The adjoining door was placed between the desk and the dresser with its TV on top, locked tight with a key card swipe on the handle. It was true he didn't have the key to it, but he doubted he'd be able to get one if he wanted it. Kathryn Spears wasn't hiding the fact that his presence was something she neither wanted nor thought she needed.

"Hey, Nikki, this is Jonathan," he said into his phone after he'd unpacked, leaving a message after the beep. "Just made first contact with Miss Scientist. Let me say, you picked one hell of a last contract for me."

Jonathan unpacked quickly, not as neatly as he'd noticed said scientist's room to be, and reflected on what he knew about the woman next door. He hadn't been lying—it wasn't much. Nikki had received the reports from the analysts and made the decision to only tell him what he needed to know in an effort to preserve some of Kathryn's privacy. What Jonathan knew was that the scientist was dedicated to her work and that work was a secret.

But that didn't mean he wasn't curious as hell as to what it entailed.

A quick knock on his door pulled him from his thoughts. He was surprised to see Kathryn standing on the other side. Her expression had softened, but only slightly.

"I want to apologize for being *frosty*," she greeted him. "I just, well, my work is a sensitive topic and this convention is very, very important for my career. My father tells me that sometimes I tend to get a little too into the zone and can lose sight of my manners." Jonathan hadn't expected an apology. "So, why don't you come with me to the Chinese restaurant a few blocks down and we can get reacquainted?"

"I appreciate the offer, but you know as part of my job I'd go anyway," he pointed out. Kathryn gave him a wry smile.

"I'm inviting you to eat *with* me," she corrected. "Not sit creepily behind me like a weird stalker."

Jonathan stepped back to retrieve his wallet and walked out into the hall. As she shut the door, he snorted.

"You apologize and then call me a stalker. I feel like you don't often apologize to people."

Kathryn crossed her arms over her chest, smile gone.

"I don't."

The walk down to the lobby and out to the street was silent. Their conversation hadn't stalled. It had stopped completely. Jonathan walked at her side but kept his eyes in a constant sweeping motion of their surroundings. It was late afternoon and the streets were packed even tighter than when he'd first driven in. Gaggles of pedestrians crowded the corners of blocks and only half waited for the Walk sign to flash green before darting across the street. Jonathan wondered if Kathryn had been to the city before. She walked with purpose and little doubt. Jonathan followed without question or comment.

Two blocks from the hotel, they hung a left into a small, one-room Chinese restaurant. It was dark and surprisingly quiet despite the street noise. The handful of patrons paid them no mind as they slid into a booth against the wall. Before they could settle in, a man took their drink orders. Jonathan checked his sight line to the door again and then decided to break his client's quiet.

"So you've been here before?" he asked, motioning around them. "Which means you've been to New York before?"

"Yes, to both. An associate who is based in Buffalo frequents a lab here and commutes just to eat the chicken fried rice when in the city." She shrugged. "Not the healthiest traveling diet, but I had to admit I was impressed the last time we ate here." Kathryn paused before smirking. "And I'm somewhat of a fast-food queen back home, so take my word for it as a weighty stamp of approval."

"Noted." The timing couldn't have been better for the waiter. He came for their orders and Jonathan decided to test out the scientist's theory. He ordered the chicken fried rice.

"So home, that's in Florida?" he asked, eyes scanning the new couple who'd just entered.

"Yes, where the humidity is king. I've lived there almost all of my life, with the exception of school."

"You moved back when finished, then?"

She nodded.

"Out of graduate school I was offered a somewhat rare job at a lab that was located near my father." She shrugged. "At the risk of sounding like a child who can't crack it without their parent nearby, I couldn't have hoped for a better setup. I love my father dearly, so back to Florida and its god-awful heat I went."

Though it was out of sight, Jonathan felt the burn of the tattoo on the back of his arm. Not a physical pain, but a memory that often flared to life when the past swarmed him.

"There's nothing wrong with staying close to family," he said, truth in each word but no experience within them.

"And what about you, Mr. Bodyguard? Where's your home?"

A simple question and one he had fielded time and time again.

"I moved around a lot growing up. Never in one place for too long." He shrugged. "When Orion started up in Dallas, I decided that I liked that city best. As someone who's traveled the world for the job, you can take my word for it 'as a weighty stamp of approval.'"

She smiled. Jonathan wondered how often she used that expression.

"Noted. You know, I've done some research of my own on Orion Security, and I must say that as a service of bodyguards, it has a fascinating track record," she began, lacing her fingers atop the table. Jonathan had wondered when she'd bring up Orion's history. He'd had no doubt that a woman whose life was so poised in research would do her own. He sat up straighter and nodded.

"We've had a few interesting cases."

"Ha! Interesting? If I recall correctly, last year one of your fellow bodyguards was instrumental in bringing down an underground drug-running organization that the police had no idea existed." Jonathan shrugged but couldn't stop the smile that sprung to his lips. The bodyguard to whom she was referring was none other than Mark Tranton. What she didn't know was that the media had been forced to keep the identity of his equal partner in crime, his now-fiancée, Kelli, and her daughter out of the public eye.

"Each case—each client—is always interesting. It's just part of the job." Kathryn seemed put off that he hadn't divulged more, but she clearly wasn't done with the topic.

"I also found a newspaper article about a woman named Morgan Avery," she said after a moment. Her expression softened just as Jonathan felt his body tense. At the moment he realized maybe he shouldn't underestimate the woman sitting across from him. While Morgan Avery was in no way a secret, it was a truth rarely connected to the agency. When he didn't respond, Kathryn took it as a sign to continue. "You used to work for Redstone Solutions, elite bodyguards, if I read their bio correctly. Morgan came to Redstone for protection but was turned away." Jonathan felt his hand start to fist. He moved it to his lap. "You quit a few weeks after she was killed."

He didn't know if it was her lack of questions that put him so suddenly on edge or if it was hearing the history of Morgan made so brief. Especially when her death had created an inexplicably vast chain of events that had so completely altered his life, as well as the lives of those he cared about most. Kathryn's eyes had narrowed a fraction. A researcher studying a subject. A scientist seeking answers. If he didn't answer in some part, he was sure she wouldn't let it go. Plus, how long had it been since he'd talked about Morgan?

"I was on a team of three. We were in the office, just having come off two back-to-back contracts, when she first came in," he started. "Young, beautiful and utterly brilliant. She was an astronomer in training who had won a spot in a prestigious program in England. It was a pretty cutthroat competition, and after she won it, she started getting threats. So bad, in fact, that she contacted us. Like you said, Redstone was viewed as a security service for the elite."

"Which translates to money, and I'm guessing she didn't have any," Kathryn supplied.

"She was a student—she had nothing to give. So she was turned down multiple times. Even when our office's secretary went to the higher-ups on her behalf. She didn't have the money. So we didn't protect her." An image of Morgan's body in a ditch, beaten almost beyond recognition, flared in his memory. Guilt and anger followed. "She was killed on the way to the airport by a man who wanted her spot. It was her original fear, and it came true."

"And then Nikki Waters founded Orion?"

It took a moment, but the chill of the past slowly heated. They'd made it to the part of the story that was no longer dripping with regret. He nodded.

"Nikki was the secretary at Redstone. After Morgan's death, she refused to work for a company that valued money over people and decided to use her contacts to create an agency that never would make that mistake again. She approached me and the team I was on and asked us to come with her." He shrugged. "So Mark, Oliver and I did. We've been there ever since."

The tattoo on the back of his arm came to the forefront of his mind. His dark mood was gone.

"You know, my mother once told me that some of the most noble pursuits begin with some of the most senseless tragedies," Kathryn said after a moment had passed. "While I don't feel I need Orion Security's protection, I see the value and heart behind what you're doing." She gave him another rarely used smile just as their food came out. Jonathan was stunned by the absolute sincerity that seemed to be behind her words. One moment she was calculated, somewhat tactless, and the next she was insightful and empathetic. Certainly one of the most interesting clients he'd had in a while.

THEY ATE THEIR food quickly and, soon after finishing, they were singing its praises.

"I'll have to let Greg know the food is still fantastic," she said. "This fast-food queen will be coming back here before I leave."

"Greg?" Jonathan asked.

"Oh, sorry. Greg is the work associate I was telling you about. If you insist on following me around the entire trip then you'll get the chance to tell him, too. I have a meeting with him tomorrow morning."

Jonathan's brows drew together.

"There was no mention in your itinerary about a meeting tomorrow," he said, most likely trying to recall the schedule she'd sent to her father, who had sent it on to Orion. Kate couldn't help it. Tension rose fast and fierce, straightening her shoulders. She pursed her lips. For a moment she'd forgotten her annoyance at the bodyguard's presence.

"That's because I didn't include it in my itinerary."

She stood and left the table to pay at the podium near the door. His next question was going to be why, and the only answer she could give would create more questions. Ones she couldn't answer.

Jonathan didn't berate her as they left the restaurant and made their way back to the hotel. In fact, he had gone silent as he trailed the space beside her, yet kept his distance. It gave her a sense of being alone. One that was shattered when he moved close with a whisper that nearly tickled her ear.

"Let's pause for a second, please."

Kate did as she was told and turned to the man, confused.

"I can see the hotel from here," she pointed out.

Jonathan grabbed her arm and pulled her backward with him. Not ready for the contact, she started to pull away when he spoke again. "I think we're being followed." His gaze cut behind her. Kate allowed him to position her so she could see the people behind them on the sidewalk. Her eyes hopscotched across each of them quickly and, she hoped, covertly. She understood the concept that if someone was following them, they would be spooked if they noticed their target noticing them.

But, then again, Kate didn't think she was being followed at all.

"The couple in the green and black jackets," he added when she was coming up empty. She turned to look for the couple in question. A dark-haired man and a dark blond-haired woman, arm in arm. Kate let out a loud sigh and turned back to Jonathan.

"You mean Mr. And Mrs. All Over Each Other?" She snorted. "I don't think their interest lies anywhere other than with each other."

"They were in the restaurant and left when we did, even though their food wasn't finished."

Although Jonathan's eyes were on hers, she could tell his attention was still tracking the upcoming couple. His intensity was almost surprising and, perhaps, the reason why she did what she did next.

"You know, you're right," she said, looking back at the couple that was nearly upon them. "They might be following us." She grabbed Jonathan's hand, abruptly breaking his focus, and smiled. "So, why don't we lose them?" Without another word from her bodyguard, Kate began moving. "Let's take a detour."

Chapter Five

The scientist pulled Jonathan to the nearest crosswalk and together they surged across the road in a cloud of pedestrians. Kathryn's grip was firm while the rest of her body seemed surprisingly loose. When she looked back at him, she even had a smile across her lips. One that, again, looked odd there, but also right.

As they hit the sidewalk she kept straight, angling them down a block with a chain clothing store and a twenty-four-hour bakery. Jonathan had studied the layout of the surrounding blocks from their hotel on the plane. It would be hard to get lost unless you intended to do just that. He was comfortable with their small detour. However, his attention was still sharp, frequently looking back over his shoulder at where the couple had been.

They stayed across the road, passing over their own crosswalk to get to the next stretch of sidewalk. Maybe he had been overreacting. The man in the green jacket turned his head and met Jonathan's stare.

Maybe not.

"Mr. Bodyguard?" Kathryn said. Jonathan didn't turn until the man dropped his gaze, laughing at whatever the woman beside him had said. "Staring isn't polite."

Jonathan refocused his attention on Kate. She had slowed her clip but kept holding his hand, steering him through foot traffic. Jonathan felt her warm skin against his. It was soft in his rugged hands, which were hardened by his time with the punching bag and weights. He briefly wondered what she thought of his rough skin before quickly killing the thought. While he knew the woman wasn't thinking about the intimacy that came with holding hands, he found his focus was starting to break because of it. Instead of shaking the hand free, however, he cleared his throat and used his training to get back to what was important.

His job.

"Let's hang a right up here. If we cross the road we'll hit construction," he said.

Kathryn snorted.

"If we're being followed, we won't lose our tail that easily," she said back, dropping her voice as if the two were conspiring. "Don't tell me I've been assigned a *lazy* bodyguard."

She looked ahead with a smirk trailing her lips. She was being difficult and she knew it, teasing him while simultaneously goading him. Jonathan didn't know if he thought the attempt was amusing, considering her earlier mood covered in frost, or annoying. Either way, he wasn't about to be labeled as lazy on his last field assignment. Even if it was by a woman he was starting to guess would never be happy with his job performance.

"You're absolutely right," he said with enthusiasm. "I really need to step up my game."

Kathryn started to loosen her grip, probably feeling her sarcasm backfiring, but Jonathan held it firm. Instead of trailing behind her, he took two long strides ahead.

Now he was leading her.

Looking both ways, Jonathan tugged her across the street to the left, in between a lag in traffic. Had they both not run, they might not have made it. Despite Kate's gasp of concern, Jonathan continued parallel to the block they'd just left before coming to the intersection. He blew through it within another pocket of pedestrians until they were at the opening of a preppy clothing store. He didn't waste any time and ducked through its double doors, passing through an invisible cloud of loud cologne and expensively dressed mannequins. One thin, very tan sales associate was on them within seconds.

"Can I help you two find anything?" the young woman said, eyes dropping to their clasped hands. She raised her expertly styled eyebrow as Jonathan kept moving.

"We're just browsing."

The associate backed off, but not without a huff.

Jonathan scanned the tops of clothing racks and display tables for an exit. While he was familiar with the shops and buildings around their hotel, he didn't know their layouts once inside. This particular store was the first of several housed in a much larger mall. Another set of double doors could be seen in the back corner, leading to what looked to be a common area between the other stores.

Jonathan slowed, hesitating in his next decision. Playing into Kathryn's teasing was fun, but pulling her into a busy area just to show he wasn't a wet blanket? That was starting to toe the line that separated fun and responsibility.

However, Kathryn didn't seem to care or to be currently struggling with his internal dilemma. She took advantage of his pause to untangle her hand from his.

"Come on, Mr. Bodyguard, let's see if you can multitask."

Then she darted toward the back corner of the store and was at the common area doors before he'd even had time to process how the absence of her hand left his cold.

Kate wasn't sure what had come over her. Maybe it was belated excitement at being so close to the convention, a giant step toward realizing a goal she'd striven toward for as long as she could remember. Or maybe it was years of being cooped up in a lab finally catching up to her that had created the sudden desire to be playful. Or maybe it was the handsome, dark-haired man who had a backstory that tugged at her heartstrings, taking him from a man who was annoying to surprisingly human. Like his picture, the man definitely wasn't of the stock variety.

Kate pushed into the common area of the minimall with a grin from ear to ear. Whatever had made this mood crop up, she was still enjoying it.

"Kathryn," Jonathan called from behind. She cast him a quick glance, noting he wasn't sharing in her mirth, but kept going.

The common area had a good number of people bustling down the hall before turning into different chain stores. Kate passed a shoe store and an electronics boutique before hitting a pocket of air that smelled so delicious it grabbed her full attention. She whipped her head upward to look at the second story. Her full stomach batted the thoughts of cookies out of her head, but the escalator leading up to them made her turn on the spot. She gave her bodyguard another grin that she felt in her bones was as mischievous as she could muster and didn't stop as she walked up the escalator.

"Kathryn," he said again, warning her. But, really, what was he going to do? He wasn't her father. He wasn't her boss. He wasn't her funder.

He definitely wasn't her husband or boyfriend.

With another weird thrill of amusement, she let out a giggle that carried her along to the second story. Heavy footfalls sounded against the metal behind her as she hit the tile. Jonathan was now quickening his pace. So, what was a girl to do?

Kate matched and then added some speed of her own. Walking fast turned into sprinting, weaving through the shoppers with nothing more than a few nasty faces and words thrown her way. She didn't care.

Now she had a mission. She was going to lose her body-guard to prove to him that, even if his intentions were good, they weren't needed.

She could lose her imaginary tail.

She could outsmart a man trained in surveillance.

She could take care of herself.

The humor she'd been feeling hardened into deter-mination.

Kate spotted an opportunity to slip out of Jonathan's view when a group of laughing teen girls exited a cof-fee shop. She cut to the right of them and immediately ducked behind their group, moving toward the second escalator that led to the first floor. When she righted herself, already descending downward, she looked over her shoulder at the bodyguard.

It worked!

Jonathan kept going straight, slowing but not stop-ping as he tried to get his eyes on her. The flush of suc-cess at evading her guard narrowed her focus as she hurried down the last of the escalator. Sure, she'd just proven she could get away, but how far could she go?

Instead of hurrying to the first-floor main entrance that deposited shoppers back to the sidewalk, Kate saw a second opportunity she couldn't pass up. Past the public bathrooms at the end of a short hall at the corner of the building were two large metal doors that must have been primarily used for bringing in merchandise. A rubber doorstop kept the door ajar. Beyond that she could see a strip of daylight. Kate booked it as fast as she could without her shoes slapping the tile too loudly, straight to and through the door.

It was the end of the mall, the building and the one next to it separated by the small walkway that ran the width of both. A set of industrial Dumpsters and their stench filled the small space, making her escape less ideal than she'd hoped it would be. But, then again, Kate didn't much care.

She'd just outsmarted her bodyguard and his tailored knowledge of keeping tabs on people.

Kate finally slowed and walked at a leisurely pace down the small alley and back to the sidewalk that ran in front of the mall's entrance. She half expected to see Jonathan blocking her path, huffing and ready to call her father, but as she scanned the faces she didn't find his.

Kate froze.

Her muscles seized, her breath held.

While she'd expected to see the bodyguard, she hadn't expected to see another face she recognized. In fact, two faces she recognized.

The couple that had originally spooked Jonathan, starting Kate's fun little exercise, were not only walking out of the mall, but doing so quickly. Like they too were in a hurry. This need seemed to intensify as the man looked to the left and the woman looked to the right, also seemingly scanning faces in the crowd.

And then the woman stopped when she locked on to a familiar face.

Hers.

Suddenly Kate cursed her game of cat and mouse with the bodyguard. The woman turned back to the man, but Kate didn't wait to see what happened next. She backtracked in record time to the alley and hurried down its length as the sound of pounding drew nearer.

Was the couple really running after her?

Why?

Was she just overreacting?

Or had Jonathan been right about the couple all along?

Kate reached the metal door that led back into the mall and started to second-guess herself. It was a co-incidence. That was all. It was perfectly normal for a couple to eat and then go shopping. It was New York City, after all. She nodded to herself, trying to ignore the fear that had cropped up. She took a step back and looked toward the mouth of the alley.

Seconds later the woman and her green jacket came into view. Kate's blood ran cold but her feet stayed warm. She grabbed the door handle, ready to fling it open and make a mad dash inside, when it swung wide so fast that she gave a little scream.

"Whoa, it's me," said Jonathan. He grabbed her shoulders, steadying her. Relief didn't just pool within her, it flooded. "What's wrong?"

Kate turned back to the mouth of the alley. The woman and her counterpart were nowhere to be seen.

"She was just there," Kate whispered.

"Who?" Jonathan's grip tightened. He moved her around behind him, looking where she had.

Maybe Kate *had* imagined it.

"Who?" he asked again. "Kathryn?"

"Call me Kate," she whispered. She shook her head and looked up at him. Embarrassment at acting like such a carefree child washed over her. While trying to avoid the bodyguard and what she believed to be a service she didn't need, she'd just managed to convince herself that she was in some kind of danger. She was creating fictional scenarios and problems for herself, most likely seeing more in the couple's actions than was there. Still, the fear wasn't fully leaving, either. Fear often led to loss of control.

And Kate didn't like losing what little control she had.

She cleared her throat before continuing with a much stronger voice. "I never liked being called Kathryn."

"Okay, *Kate*," he started, brows pulling together. "Who did you see?"

"Never mind," she said. She straightened her back and took a deep breath. There was no way she was going to let the bodyguard's paranoia and her fear make her lose her focus. "Let's head back," she said, no longer wanting to explore.

Kate might be able to write off how the woman in the green coat had seemingly been looking for her as a coincidence, but she wasn't about to take off from the bodyguard's side again.

She was in denial, but not *that* much.

THE WALK BACK to the hotel was quiet. More than anything Jonathan wanted to reprimand his charge for running off, but after seeing her expression in the alley, he'd refrained. Whatever—whoever—she'd seen had spooked her. While seeing Jonathan had done the opposite.

She'd let out a deep sigh that had seemingly passed through her entire body at the sight of him. Seeing such poignant relief because of his proximity had affected him almost as much as the look of fear she'd harbored seconds before. The absurd amount of annoyance he'd felt for Kathryn—*Kate*—had taken a backseat to a resounding protectiveness that went beyond his usual job duties.

He suddenly not only needed to keep her safe, he *wanted* to do it, and to the best of his abilities.

The silence stretched past the sidewalk and up to their rooms, and when it finally broke, it wasn't by much.

"I'm a little tired from traveling," Kate muttered. "I'll let you know if I want to leave." There was an undercurrent to her words, but Jonathan couldn't place the emotion creating it. Was it guilt at ditching him earlier? Or residual fear from whatever had happened when he hadn't been right on her heels?

"Thank you," was all he could say.

She nodded and opened her door. He waited until it was closed and the top latch was thrown in place. It made him wonder if she'd done it by habit, or if Kate was more worried than she was letting on.

Chapter Six

Kate closed the top latch over the door and took a step back to look at it. She heard Jonathan's door close.

You aren't in any danger, she thought. *Don't let his overprotectiveness worry you.*

But even as she gave herself the advice, she couldn't help but feel an influx of nerves tighten her stomach.

"This is why I didn't want a bodyguard," she muttered, rubbing her stomach. "Now I think I have problems I don't really have."

Trying to forget about the man next door wasn't as easy as she'd hoped.

Talking about his past, including Orion's origin, had softened her otherwise harsh opinion of the man. He wasn't some faceless hunk of meat sent to stalk her in hopes of keeping a potentially imaginary predator at bay. He was a man who had persevered through tragedy and had made a life of preventing it from repeating again.

And wasn't that exactly what she was doing, too?

She tried to banish thoughts of the brooding dark-haired man and fell onto the bed. The jaunt right after eating a full meal plus traveling combined to make her eyelids unbelievably heavy as soon as she hit the pillow.

The feeling of exhaustion and the desire to give in to the comfort of the bed surprised her. Taking naps wasn't something she was used to doing. In the last few years, if there was time to sleep, then that meant there was time to work. She'd rarely picked a nap over lab time. It was a choice that had turned into a habit.

A yawn tore itself from her lips and she knew it wouldn't be long before she was asleep.

This trip was already turning out much differently than she had originally planned.

THE ROOM WAS DARK.

Barely any light filtered in from behind the curtains. It was so dim Kate placed them as streetlights. Which meant her nap had stretched longer than she'd meant it to.

She rolled onto her back and yawned. Even though she'd been sleeping, she felt exhaustion still weighing her down. If she closed her eyes again, she was sure she'd sleep until morning.

So what had woken her up?

She tilted her head, listening.

A car horn blared outside, promptly followed by two more.

Ah, the sweet sounds of New York City, she thought.

She contemplated her next move, listening to a symphony of agitated drivers vent via their respective vehicles when another sound caught her ear.

Confused, she turned her head, peering into the dark for the culprit. It stopped.

Kate's heartbeat began to pick up. She waited. There it was again.

Someone was in the hallway.

But what were they doing?

Curious—always curious—Kate got off the bed and made her way to the door. She peered through the peephole but was met with a cloudy circle with no help identifying who was outside. If there was anyone at all. She dropped back down to flat-footed and bit her bottom lip, waiting.

Seconds turned into minutes. Kate remained perfectly still until she was positive the sound, whatever it had been, had stopped. Slowly she unlatched the top lock and eased the door open a crack.

No one was there.

Cautious, Kate stepped out into the hallway. It was empty. She let out a breath she hadn't realized she was holding.

See? That bodyguard has made you paranoid, she thought. *No one is after you. No one even knows where you—*

Her current thought bubble popped as she turned.

Taped to the door was a piece of paper with a single word written on it: *Stop*.

However, it wasn't the message that made her throat catch.

Soaking the paper, blurring the one bold word, was blood. It ran off the paper and down the chipped paint of the door.

And this time, Kate didn't think it was fake.

Chapter Seven

Jonathan was barely out of the shower when a pounding sounded against his door. Adrenaline spiked at the urgency behind each knock. He dropped the towel to his waist and had the door open within seconds, water dripping off him and on to the carpet.

"I think it's real," Kate greeted. She was still wearing her clothes from earlier but the impression of a pillow lined the right side of her face while her hair was ruffled. Like he'd suspected, she had been sleeping for the last few hours. Her expression, however, was not in the least rested. Her brows were pushed together, a wrinkle between them, and she wore a frown so pronounced it seemed to drag down every line that made up her face.

"What?" Jonathan asked, an umbrella question to everything.

"This time I think it's real," she repeated.

"What's real?" Jonathan moved closer, out of the doorway. He was trying to get an answer that made sense. What he got was Kate's shaky hand pointing to her door.

And then he understood.

"It's real blood," he said, senses going on alert as he took in what was taped to her door. This one undoubtedly looked more menacing than the other letters she'd received.

"Yes. The coloring, the way it drips," she added. "The way it smells."

Jonathan didn't need to sniff the dark crimson to agree with her assessment. When he was a teenager, he'd gotten into a bad fight with a kid in foster care over which bed was his. The kid had been older and bigger and had hit Jonathan so perfectly in the nose that he busted it on impact. For nearly an hour it had bled. The color and consistency matched what was on the door now.

That was real blood, all right.

"Did you see who put it here?" he asked. His head swiveled back and forth down the empty hallway.

"No. I heard something and when I came out here to look I found—" she motioned to the note, eyes wide "—that."

Jonathan spotted the bubble cameras at each end of the hall.

"I bet those did," he muttered. "Have you touched it in any way?"

Kate shook her head.

"I just saw it and then knocked on your door."

"Good, come on."

He motioned for her to go into his room. Her concerned look turned stubborn immediately.

"Shouldn't we call someone?"

"We will, but inside the room," he said, holding back a building tidal wave of frustration only she seemed to be able to produce within him. "If you haven't noticed, the longest trail of blood hasn't even made it to the carpet yet."

Kate whipped her head back to the door and he knew when she saw what he was talking about.

"Which means—" Jonathan started before she cut him off.

"That it hasn't been there long at all."

"A plus for the scientist," he said, waving her through again.

This time she followed instructions without resistance.

"Call the front desk and get the manager up here," he said, following her in and immediately going to his still-packed bag. "Let them know that you're also calling the cops." Kate's mouth opened and closed, like a fish out of water. "Listen, there's no doubt in my mind this letter is connected to the others you've been receiving. Which means his anger is escalating." He held up his fingers to tick off his points as he made them. "One large 'stop' instead of a page filled with the word. Real blood, not fake. On your hotel-room door, states away from home. Even that stubborn brain of yours has to see that whoever is behind these letters is getting angrier."

He watched as the urge to fight back—to be the one making complete sense—flashed across her face. Thankfully, it disappeared quickly. In its place was the face of a woman who finally agreed with him. She nodded.

"Which asks the question...what's next?"

"Let's make sure we never have to find out. Now call the front desk and, if you don't want to see me naked, turn around."

Jonathan saw her cheeks redden, but he didn't have time to dwell on it. Someone had left a letter soaked in blood as a warning to Kate—a violent threat. Jonathan not only wanted to protect her from that person, he wanted to find and stop them, too.

He changed into a white T-shirt and covered it with a gray button-down and a pair of khakis that were a bit tighter than he liked thanks to his recently changed leg workouts. Once he put on his boots, though, he wasn't thinking about how his clothes looked. His mind was already focused outside the hotel room.

"The front-desk guy, Jett, the one who checked you in, said a manager is on the way up," Kate said, eyes still averted. "He sounded more than concerned."

"Good, he should be."

Jonathan grabbed his cell phone and rummaged through his bags until he found something he had hoped he wouldn't even have to think about while on contract.

"Orion prides itself on always trying to use nonlethal means to protect our clients," he said, walking to the other side of the bed where Kate sat with the phone. "But since you refused a second bodyguard and now you're getting bloody letters on your door, I'm going to give you this and warn you to be careful." Jonathan extended the small block of plastic to her. It was black with a strip of school-bus yellow across the grips on either side and about as heavy as it looked. "Do I need to show you how to use it?"

Kate's eyes had widened when she realized what it was, but the surprise didn't last long.

"I'm a woman who lives by herself," she said, taking it carefully and placing it on the nightstand. "I know how to use a Taser, Mr. Bodyguard."

"Good to know, Miss Scientist," he said, resisting the urge to roll his eyes at her. "Now call the police and don't open this door until I come back."

"Where are you going?"

"To find out who left that note," he said, already at the door and opening it. "And to find out how they knew exactly what room you were in."

THE MANAGER WAS a woman named Lola Teague and she was as concerned as she was determined to help. She met Jonathan at the elevator, sporting a dark navy pantsuit, heels and a name tag that caught the fluorescent lights. Jonathan placed Lola in her fifties, with impeccably styled dark hair, matching pristine posture and laugh lines at the corners of her eyes.

When she saw the note on the door, she definitely wasn't laughing.

She let out a low whistle.

"This is a first for us. And that says something, coming from someone who has been with the hotel since day one." She leaned in close but was careful not to touch, a consideration that made Jonathan instantly respect her. "To be perfectly candid, where other managers might want to call the hotel owner before the cops, I don't share the same school of thought." She straightened and gave him a severe look.

"Don't worry, we already called."

Lola gave a quick nod before giving him an appraising look.

"You're the bodyguard, then?" she asked before tacking on, "Jett heard the two of you talking when you checked in earlier."

Jonathan's jaw tightened.

"I hope he wasn't broadcasting our stay here," he said, voice dangerously low. "Because, I'll be candid, too—very few people knew we were staying at this hotel. We haven't been here for more than a few hours and someone knows exactly what room she was in."

Lola didn't miss the implication that Jett might have told someone where they could be found. He saw her tense up. Professional distress.

Welcome to my world, he thought.

Instead of trying to defend her employee, however, her eyes flitted down the hall. He followed her gaze to the security camera.

"I think it's time to see what our cameras picked up."

"I think you're right."

Jonathan paused to take a picture of the note and door before following the manager into the elevator and down to the lobby. Jett sat at the front desk, eyes darting to each new face that entered. Jonathan was doing the same thing, though he hoped a little more slyly than the young black-haired man. His head jerked around like he was on a roller coaster.

"Jett," Lola greeted, voice as even as it had been when she had spoken upstairs. "Did you by chance tell anyone that Miss Spears or Mr. Carmichael were staying here?"

"Or mention which rooms?" Jonathan added.

Jett's eyes widened a fraction but he didn't sag with guilt or pucker up with resentment at the question.

"No way," he exclaimed to them. He turned to Jonathan. "You were the only one who even asked about her. No one else has called or come to me asking about either one of you. Especially not room numbers. I swear!"

Lola gave a curt nod and shared a look with Jonathan. One that asked if he was satisfied with her employee's answer, because she was.

"Okay," Jonathan consented.

"Jett, please come get us when the police arrive," she said. "Also, send Norman up there to make sure no one touches that letter until the cops get here."

"Yes, ma'am."

"Norman?" Jonathan asked.

"The head of our cleaning staff," she answered before addressing Jett again.

"And Jett? If you see *anyone*, and I mean *anyone*,

you don't recognize as a guest, come get me immediately."

Jett nodded and went back to hawk-eyeing each guest who walked past.

Lola led them around the front desk to a door in the corner marked Employees Only. It opened up into a small hall that forked right up to another door. It was marked Security. The manager got a key out and unlocked the door.

"I just realized," she said, not at all happy, "whoever put up that note did so during our security guard Bernie's dinner break. What are the odds?"

"Who says it's a coincidence?" Jonathan pointed out. Lola paused a moment, taking in his meaning, before pushing into the small room. Whatever was happening, Jonathan wasn't liking it one bit. Escalating threats, obvious malice and now a coincidence like the one guard supposed to watch the security camera just happened to be on break when the note was delivered?

This contract—protecting Kate Spears—had taken a turn he hadn't anticipated at all.

The security room wasn't much to look at. A desk ran the length of the wall with two flat-screen monitors on top. Eight frames were displayed within each.

"This is your floor," Lola pointed out, sitting down in the desk chair. "What one camera caught, so did the other." Jonathan came closer and looked at the real-time feed. Kate's door was square in the middle of the two, close enough that anyone who went up to it would be seen but far enough away that the note on the door wasn't as noticeable. Even the blood.

Lola clicked around the computer while Jonathan's attention roamed over the rest of the live security feeds. There was not a lot of movement and, even if there had been, it wasn't like he could question each and every guest in hopes he'd get lucky and catch the culprit. He had a feeling it wouldn't be *that* easy.

"How far back should I go?" she asked, both of the hall's feeds the only images on one monitor.

"Try fifteen minutes."

She did as he said and they watched as three different people moved down the hall and into their respective rooms. Not one of them stopped at Kate's door.

"Go back a few more minutes."

Lola started to move the frames back by five minutes when Jonathan held out his hand.

"There," he said. "He's in front of her door."

The two quieted as she hit Play. They watched as a man took out what looked like a large plastic sandwich bag from beneath his jacket.

"That's the paper on her door," Lola said.

Jonathan nodded.

"He had it in a bag so the blood wouldn't get everywhere."

The man carefully took the note out, not at all worried that someone might see him. He pressed the paper against the door. With his free hand he produced a roll of duct tape and yanked off a piece. If Jonathan hadn't been in the shower, he surely would have heard that.

Like he was hanging a birthday banner, the man taped the blood-soaked paper to the door. When he was satisfied that it would stay up, he turned and began to walk away.

Lola paused that particular frame.

"I'm going to print this out," she said, already doing just that. Jonathan didn't respond. All of his attention was on the man's face. Anger, hot and fluid, moved over every inch of his skin. "Wait," Lola said, pausing in what she was doing to look back at him. "Do you know this man?"

"No," he admitted. "I saw him earlier today, though. He had a woman with him then."

But, what Jonathan really wanted to know was, where were they now?

Chapter Eight

Kate rubbed her arms as if the motion would scrub away the feeling of unease that had crept in. The two NYPD officers who had shown up had eyed the bloody threat with a good dose of concern, but it hadn't lasted long. They took pictures, removed the letter and bagged it.

"We'll check the blood to see who or what it belongs to," one of them said. "If anything comes up, we'll let you know."

Kate watched as Jonathan's mood darkened. He had expected more.

"And the man?" he asked when the two looked like they were ready to leave.

"We'll run his name and pay him a visit," the most senior of the two said. "What happens during that visit depends on if this is real blood or not."

They didn't stick around past that. Kate watched them walk down the narrow hallway to the elevators with a flush of frustration she'd bet the bodyguard was also harboring.

"I thought they'd be more helpful, somehow," she admitted when the officers were in the elevator. "They didn't really even seem to be too concerned about it. I mean, I know they've probably seen much worse than a blood-soaked letter, but still…"

Jonathan muttered something angrily beneath his breath before motioning to her door.

"Go ahead and get your things together."

Kate's eyebrows flew straight up.

"What? We aren't leaving," she exclaimed. "I don't care if some sadistic person is trying their best to freak me out. I have work to do and I'm not—"

"Kate," Jonathan interrupted. He held his hand up to further emphasize the need for her to stop. "I had a feeling you wouldn't leave, even if I asked. The hotel manager is letting us move to another set of rooms off book."

Kate felt her face heat slightly.

"Oh."

"Yeah, so please go get your things together so we can go to our new rooms."

Kate nodded, but paused before opening her door.

"What do you mean, 'off book'?"

"In the computers we'll still be registered as staying in these rooms. The ones we'll be using are now booked under different names. Hopefully that will keep our letter writer from paying us another visit." He quieted a moment. "I don't think they will rebook this room on the off chance the writer decides to escalate, either. Also, may I point out that you *should* care that some sadistic person is trying their best to freak you out. Caution isn't for stupid people, Kate. It's smart people who've realized that they should be careful."

Kate felt the low thrum of nerves in her stomach get a touch louder. She nodded to Jonathan and his words of wisdom, and again she wondered what that next step might be. Either way, Jonathan wasn't taking any chances. He waited for her to go inside and lock her door before she heard him go to his own room.

Packing quickly made the methodical side of her cringe. What normally would have her taking her time—finding each article of clothing and accessory a specific place—had her cramming her luggage full. The room, she realized, now felt tainted in a way. Whose blood had been on that letter? Was it the man she'd seen earlier on the street? Or had he taken it from someone else?

Kate's eyes traveled to the side pocket of her bag. Within it was a small leather-bound notebook.

What you're doing is important, Kate, she thought. *Don't let them scare you.*

She took a deep breath.

Jonathan was already packed and waiting for her in the hall when she finished. Without a word he took the bag from her and began walking. She gave the door one last look. The hotel manager had said she would be cleaning it off personally. Kate hoped she'd do it soon, or some late nighters would get more of a scare than they'd bargained for.

"We need to talk more about tonight," Jonathan said

as soon as the elevator doors closed them in. Kate followed his finger as he hit the third-floor button. She didn't want to look him in the eyes. She didn't want to fight.

"Aren't bodyguards supposed to be quiet observers?" she asked with a small smile. Even though she'd taken a nap earlier, fatigue was pulling her body down. Her adrenaline had spiked when she'd seen the present left on the door. Now it had all but worn off, leaving exhaustion in its wake. She didn't want to talk about any of it right then. Not even with the man who was obviously trying his best to keep her safe without knowing whom he was protecting her from.

"I thought you didn't like men who quietly watched you from a distance." Though the reference was done in a humorous way, Kate detected no lightness to his mood. She cut her eyes toward him.

Looking straight ahead, there was no denying Jonathan Carmichael had an absolutely handsome profile. Hard angles to his jaw, chin and nose gave him a sculpted, tough look, while his eyes...

Jonathan turned and met her stare with his own. Those very eyes she'd just been trying to find descriptors for were now focused squarely on her.

Kate prided herself on being meticulous in work and in life. She labeled things—and people—with no second thoughts. She paid attention to the smaller details while often losing sight of the larger picture, as her father liked to say. To know the name of something—the essence of what made it up—was a natural and necessary ritual for her. A reflex of sorts that had made her work life flourish while, perhaps, stunting her personal one. Her emotions were included in the latter. Kate wouldn't go as far as to say she didn't have feelings— she did—but they were calculated and timed with reason.

Yet, in that moment, Kate found a part of her floundering to make sense of a new warmth that had taken place within her. What's more, in all of her vocabulary and thought, she couldn't seem to find one word to describe the dark blue of her bodyguard's eyes.

And certainly not how they made her feel all of a sudden.

"Are you okay?" he asked, the world beneath their feet stopping. The elevator beeped. The door slid open. "Kate?" His voice dipped low, concern clearly there. She'd known him for less than a day and here he was, showing genuine concern for her well-being. Was that just part of the job?

Kate blinked.

"Sorry. I just—I'm tired. I guess I was more worn out from traveling than I'd thought." To prove her point, she stifled a yawn, stretching her arms out wide. "Don't you want to get some sleep?" Jonathan held her stare a moment longer before she slid into the hallway, trying to escape whatever fog she'd just found herself in. Why would it matter if he cared for her beyond his bodyguard duties? Or if he didn't? Kate didn't detest the idea that Jonathan could genuinely care. Instead it created an anxious feeling inside her. What would she even do if he did?

"I've learned to operate on little sleep," he said matter-of-factly, following her out. "Call it a trick of the trade."

They moved down the hall and to their new rooms, Jonathan unlocking the first before going inside. He did the same sweep he'd done that morning, checking every inch of the space before giving it the okay. When he was finished, however, he went to the door and threw the top latch.

Locking the two of them inside.

The fog from earlier rushed back, but this time lightning jolted through it. Heat rose up her neck and spread to her cheeks. She raised her eyebrow, questioning the man. Was he staying the night with her?

Quickly her eyes flitted to the one king-size bed in the room. Her skin grew hotter.

If Jonathan noticed her burning blush, he didn't say anything.

"I know you're not a fan of adjoining rooms," he said, walking to the one next to her. "But given what's happened, I thought it might be smart to have access to one." He pulled another key card from his pocket and slid it into the lock on the door. It clicked and he opened it wide. Kate peered in to see another duplicate room. One with its own king-size bed.

The heat that should have abated at realizing the bodyguard wasn't trying to stay in her room didn't. Kate turned to her bag on the floor and unzipped it, talking over her shoulder while she hoped her face wasn't too red.

"As long as you don't decide to turn into a creep and come into my room while I sleep, I think I'll survive."

He laughed.

"I won't come stare at you sleeping if you don't do the same to me." She turned as he placed a second key card on the TV stand next to the door. "If you need me, just knock. Good night."

He started to close his door when Kate moved toward him. He stopped as she called his name.

"Jonathan?" He turned and once again she was slammed with the full impact of his eyes. She didn't let it divert her current thought process, though. "I don't know exactly how Orion and its agents work—if you call in and give updates—but I'd really appreciate it if you wouldn't mention to my father what's happened." She gave him a small smile. "I know technically he's the one who hired you, but he worries too much."

The bodyguard looked like he was going to say something but decided against it. He didn't return her smile.

"You know, it's okay to have people worry about you. That's all some people want in this world." The way he said the last part pulled at her heart. It also piqued her curiosity about the life of the man in front of her. Regardless, she pressed on.

"My father has had enough worry to last him a lifetime," she said. "I don't want to add to it until I have to."

She searched his face, looking for the cause of the hardened man.

"When this is over, I'll give a full report to my boss and then she'll debrief the client. But, for now, I think we both need some sleep."

It wasn't a yes to her request, but it wasn't a no, either.

No THREATENING LETTERS covered in blood appeared during the night. The hotel's day manager, a balding man named Ted, kept a vigilant eye out for the man caught on the security footage as well as any other suspicious activity after Lola explained what had happened. Like Jett, his enthusiasm worked to their advantage. It was like he'd been asked to be a spy temporarily. He seemed to enjoy a break from his normal, everyday activities.

When Kate and Jonathan came down to the lobby to introduce themselves, he was more than accommodating.

"If you'd like to have breakfast, it's on the house," he chirped at them. Kate's stomach growled in response. She hadn't eaten since the Chinese restaurant the day before.

"That's nice," she commented. Ted in turn kept smiling even as he leaned in close to ask for any updates from the police.

"I called in before we came down but was told there was no new information," Jonathan answered with a shrug. "I suppose we just have to wait."

Ted nodded to that, and Kate and the bodyguard

took advantage of their free breakfast. It wasn't until they were halfway into their eggs and bacon that the man across from her asked a question she'd been expecting.

"So, what exactly is this convention all about?"

Kate paused her fork in midair.

"What do you know about it already?" she asked, curious.

"Nothing other than you need to be invited and wear something nice."

Kate smirked.

"The convention, typically, isn't a public affair. Depending on your field of study, what you're working on and your connections, you get invited to showcase your research or invention. You basically present to potential sponsors for funding." She felt her smirk transform into a more genuine show of excitement. "I had a breakthrough with the work I've been doing and was invited to present my research." Jonathan nodded, seemingly impressed. If he wanted more details than that, he was going to be disappointed. Only those who needed to know did. "That's actually why we're meeting Greg for coffee. He's more of a mentor and, I'm hoping, has a present for me."

Jonathan raised his eyebrow.

"What kind of present?" he asked.

Her smirk came back in full.

"The game-changing kind."

Chapter Nine

Greg Calhoun was short, round and had little hair. His dark skin was a complete contrast to his chemically treated white smile, and his glasses were as awkwardly shaped as the crumpled handkerchief he always carried in his pocket. He entered the coffee shop with a narrow focus that didn't dissipate until his eyes landed on Kate. He shone his sparkling smile and made a beeline for her.

"Kate," he exclaimed in greeting. "What a sight for sore eyes."

Kate stood and accepted his embrace. She felt the corners of her lips lift. Her social life might have been stunted by her professional one, but she considered the older man a true friend.

"Nice to see you, too, Greg. It's been a long time since we've talked to each other in person," she said, sitting back down. Jonathan sat to her left and extended a hand to Greg as he sat opposite. "Greg, I'd like to introduce you to Jonathan Carmichael." Kate hesitated before explaining their relationship. She hadn't told anyone aside from a friend about her father's need for his daughter to be protected. Was it against the rules to tell him now that Jonathan was her bodyguard? She trusted Greg. Few people in her life had garnered such intense trust and loyalty from her. Shouldn't she pay him the same courtesy?

"I'm her bodyguard." Jonathan spoke up while she was still deciding what to say. Surprised, she tilted her head. "You seemed to be struggling with what to label me," he whispered before turning back to the man.

Greg shook his hand without issue and nodded.

"I'm glad you hired one, to be honest," he said. "Once your father told me about the letters, I was concerned you weren't being cautious enough."

Kate's eyes widened and a slow burn crept to her face.

"My father told you about the letters?" she asked. Greg paid her enough respect to look sheepish.

"He phoned me after he found out. I think he made the call to find out if I sent them or had received any like them. When he was convinced I really hadn't known about their existence, he told me to keep an eye out for you at the convention." He patted his pronounced stomach and then motioned to Jonathan's flat front. "I'm glad you decided to get someone a bit more qualified."

Jonathan let out a small laugh, but Kate wasn't in the mood. Her father had gone behind her back. She could already imagine the unapologetic look on Deacon's face when she eventually confronted him about it.

"Listen, don't be mad at your father," Greg added.

"He's worried about you and—" he put the silver case he'd been carrying on the table and gave it a pat "—I don't blame him."

Despite the subtle warning, Kate couldn't help but grin.

"You actually got it," she almost yelled in excitement. Suddenly the anxiety of the last twenty-four hours disappeared. "I was worried it wouldn't be ready in time!"

Greg smiled.

"You may not be able to use it, but I think it will help to have at least one physical example of the work you've been doing. Seeing is believing and all of that." He pulled the case off the table and set it on the ground beside him. Jonathan looked between the two without saying a thing. If it had been Kate, she would have questioned the exchange, but she had a feeling Jonathan was staying professional. He was there to guard her, not nose into her business. Again, something she definitely would have been doing if the shoe had been on the other foot.

"Well, thank you," she said. "Hopefully this will get people's attention."

Greg sobered slightly.

"I hope so." He turned to Jonathan and gave him a sly smile. "Speaking of hope, I hope this one here hasn't made your life too difficult. I know she can be a handful."

Jonathan laughed.

"She's not the most difficult client I've had," he answered. "She's not the easiest, either."

Greg gave a hoot of laughter.

"I'm right here, you know," Kate pointed out. Jonathan cut her a quick smirk. It jump-started parts of her she hadn't realized needed jump-starting. Once again, warmth started to spread up her chest and neck. She hid behind her coffee, taking a big swig. Had he been this attractive when they'd first met? Or had she been too distracted by her disgruntled attitude to really feel it?

"That's a very politically correct way to phrase it," Greg said. His expression softened. "Cassandra was the same way. She liked to say she was just spirited. Kathryn here definitely could fall into the same category." Kate lowered her cup. Her mother's name impacted her in two ways every time she was mentioned. She remembered the woman who had loved her and whom she had loved back. Cassandra's inspiring compassion and untouchable determination had left a lasting mark on her only daughter. Kate felt the same love she'd felt all those years ago every time the woman was brought up. Yet, at the same token, she also felt the emptiness her death had left behind. A blank space that should have been filled with memories of growing up with her. Memories that should have included school dances and birthday parties, teenage love problems that only moms knew how to fix, graduations and celebrations, quiet nights spent watching TV together, oblivious to the pain that would be felt if all of it were to be taken away.

Greg reached forward and patted the top of Kate's hand. He wasn't a stranger to the pain that Cassandra Spears's death had brought. Jonathan once again remained quiet, obviously trying to respect the turn in conversation. He searched her face, though, as if there was something in her eyes that could lead him to the answer. In the moment, she felt an odd sense of obligation to him.

"Greg used to work with my mother when she needed some scientific expertise for her job. He became a family friend," she explained after clearing her throat. "When he found out about my research, he reached out and helped me connect with my current lab and secure start-up funding. He's had an integral part in how I got to where I am now."

"Sounds like a good man to have on your side," Jonathan observed. Kate nodded.

"One of the best!"

Greg put his hands up, smiling.

"And here I thought I was just coming to deliver a package, not have my praises sung among the smell of roasting coffee beans and budding writers working on their screenplays." They glanced over to a younger man with bright blue hair, head bent over his laptop and two empty coffee cups next to him. Kate couldn't help but laugh.

"So, is what you do as secretive as what Kate does?" Jonathan asked. Apparently he could curb his curiosity for only so long.

"Not particularly," Greg said with a grin. "I used to

be an adjunct professor at Harvard—science was my game—when I decided I'd like a change of pace. I'm a business consultant now, with an unperturbed affinity for scientific pursuits on the side. That's to say, I dabble in lab work here and there, and am occasionally hired as an adviser on more complicated projects." Greg shrugged. "Mostly boring work, I'm sure, especially compared to the life of a bodyguard."

Jonathan cracked a smile.

"It has its moments. The travel is great and the people I've met have been—" he gave Kate a pointed glance "—interesting."

"I'd imagine so! It sounds like a dream job for some."

Jonathan's smile at talking about his job—one he seemed to hold very dear—lost some of its mirth. The corners dropped slightly.

"It used to be mine," he admitted. "But, actually, this is my last field contract."

That caught Kate off guard.

"You're leaving Orion?"

Jonathan shook his head.

"I'm not leaving Orion unless Nikki Waters tells me to," he said with a laugh. "Until then she's agreed to help find me a job at the office. One where I'm not constantly traveling."

"Roots," was all Greg said, as if all of his wisdom leaked into the one syllable. Jonathan nodded. The two men shared a look of what Kate believed to be understanding. She, however, hadn't yet caught the meaning behind it. If Jonathan loved his job so much, why give it up for a glorified desk job?

"So does that mean you have someone back home you'd like to grow those roots with?" Kate's idea about questioning why a seemingly driven man like Jonathan would give up fieldwork came to a screeching halt. Since she'd met the bodyguard, she hadn't once asked him about or even pondered his relationship status. She hadn't seen a ring on his finger and had assumed he wasn't married, but beyond that she'd not thought about it. Not even when realizing how attracted to him she was.

Jonathan's weakening smile found a dose of strength. It grew alongside a sinking, cold feeling of disappointment in Kate. Why?

Why did it matter if he had someone back home? He was her bodyguard, nothing more.

"Sadly, no. Aside from friends, it's only my roots that will be growing." The cold in Kate's stomach found a spot to settle. Greg's eyes swept her expression and once again she hid behind her coffee cup.

"I'm sure you'll find someone to share your life with," Greg said. Then, with another loud hoot of laughter he added, "And if not, you could always get a dog."

Both men burst into a fit of laughter. One Kate found herself joining in on. She'd been unsure of how this meeting would go. Greg was and always had been a nice man. However, like her, there were moments when he'd become clipped and detached, his thoughts trailing back to whatever project he was currently on. Kate was glad Jonathan was able to meet the carefree and personable Greg Calhoun. For some reason, she found she wanted the bodyguard to like him. And vice versa.

"Well, Kathryn, it's only fair I reiterate the same question to you," Greg said once their laughter had died off. "I know we talk a lot, but it's been a while since the topic centered on anything other than work. Are you still dating that man? What's his name?"

Kate felt her cheeks heat. She cast a quick look at Jonathan, who seemed to be paying rapt attention. His dark blue eyes were honed in on her face. She guessed she wasn't the only one who had been in the dark about the other's romantic attachments.

"If you mean Caleb, and I'm pretty sure you do, then no," she admitted. "We didn't make it past year two of the project." Three years later and she hadn't dated, let alone been interested in, anyone since. Though she thought she had filled Greg in on the matter since then, she wasn't surprised she hadn't. When they spoke on the phone it was all about research and data and theories. Not their love lives. She shrugged before either man could comment. "More time to work, if you ask me."

Greg reached out and patted her hand against the coffee cup again, mouth opening to say something she'd bet would be profound, when Jonathan spoke up instead.

"You know what they say about all work and no

play." Kate's breath caught just as Jonathan gave her a wink. For a moment all she could do was stare.

"I like you, Jonathan," Greg said. "Which is another reason I hate to say I need to leave." He started to stand and Kate and Jonathan followed suit. "I'm currently working on a project that requires my close attention."

"Well, thank you for coming to meet me," Kate said, reaching down for the silver case. "And thank you for working on this."

The three of them walked out to the sidewalk, the morning light making Kate squint as her eyes adjusted. The case was hardly heavy in her hands. Her mind had already begun to form a mental picture of what it looked like. While she'd more or less created it, she'd never seen it take a physical form.

"It was nice to meet you, Jonathan," Greg said, pausing for a handshake. "I wish you luck with growing roots, and also for keeping up with this one."

"She's spirited," Jonathan said.

Greg laughed.

"Bingo." He turned to Kate and enveloped her in a quick hug. "Your mother would be so proud of you," he whispered in her ear. "As am I."

"Thank you," she said, a different kind of warmth spreading through her. "That means a lot."

They parted and he gave her one last pat on the hand.

"Let me know if you need anything, and good luck with the convention." He gave a small nod to Jonathan, who returned it, and then started to cross the wide crosswalk toward a parking garage. Jonathan began to turn in the direction of the hotel when Kate remembered a question she needed to ask.

"Wait, I have to ask him for the code on this thing," she said, motioning to the case. Greg was already halfway across the street, surrounded by pedestrians. The Walk sign was still white.

"Greg," Kate called as she and Jonathan hit the crosswalk. He heard them and turned, pausing his stride.

Even though he didn't know why she'd called him, there was a smile pulling up his lips.

It was bright and happy and genuine.

Then the screaming started.

Chapter Ten

The car lurched forward without any indication that it was going to stop. Not even as the front bumper connected with a man and woman midstep. They didn't have time to scream as they were run over, but the pedestrians around them didn't let that stop them from yelling in terror.

The car, a few feet to their right, was merely slowed by the people it had hit. Jonathan tried to look into the driver's side through the windshield but didn't have time to focus on the face behind the wheel. The sound of a revving engine mixed with the screaming around him.

Like the fight between him and the thug during his last contract protecting Martin, Jonathan would later realize what happened next might have gone a completely different way. If he hadn't moved slightly ahead of Kate, right in between her and Greg, he never would have had enough time to pull her out of the way. As it was, he was lucky. He pivoted and slung his body into hers. His height and muscle—and her sheer surprise—

knocked the two of them out of the way just as the car continued through the crosswalk.

Arm over Kate's chest, they hit the asphalt hard. Pain burst in his side and elbow as they took the brunt of his fall, but Kate wasn't as lucky. Amid the cries around them, he was able to hear Kate's own cry of pain as her head whipped back against the road.

"Are you okay?" Jonathan yelled out, already scrambling to stand. Lying in a crosswalk while people were getting run over wasn't something he wanted them to do. Kate shut her eyes tight with another cry of pain. Her hand flew to the back of her head, and when she pulled it away it was bloody. He turned as another wave of screaming intensified. The car's back bumper was only a few inches away. They'd just missed being run over. "Kate?" he asked, turning his attention back to her, wanting to get her away from the carnage.

"My head," she said, reaching out to take his hand. He got her to her feet, barely steadying her before she yelled again.

This time it wasn't in pain.

"Greg!" Kate rocketed around Jonathan, stumbling once before making it to the man. He lay crumpled on the asphalt, unmoving and bloodied. Jonathan hurried over just as Kate dropped to her knees beside the man's head.

The car that had inflicted the damage had finally stopped, ramming into a parked car waiting for the light to change. It was immediately swarmed by angry bystanders while others were seeing to those who had been hit. From a glance around him, Jonathan counted five people lying on the ground.

Kate grabbed Greg's wrist, checking for a pulse. A woman who had missed the car's path through the crosswalk caught Jonathan's attention.

"He didn't go under. He bounced off the side."

Jonathan knew that was good. Better than being run over and crushed. But the way Kate's entire body fell as she fished for the man's pulse made him believe maybe that one saving grace hadn't been enough.

"No, no, no, no, no," she whispered in quick procession. "Please, Greg, please!"

Jonathan was about to kneel to check the man out when a yell grabbed his attention.

"She's running!"

He turned to watch as the driver got out of the car and punched the first person next to her door. She threw another few hits to get the people around her to step back long enough to make a break for the sidewalk. It was then that he got a good look at her.

It was the woman who had been following them the day before, arm bandaged and expression determined.

Jonathan half expected the man who had left the letter to get out of the passenger side to join her, but the door never opened.

"It's her," Jonathan yelled to Kate, rage building in his system. Surely it was no coincidence she of all people had driven a car that nearly killed them.

No, it couldn't be a coincidence.

Kate looked up to see what he meant and realization

washed over her face. That was all Jonathan needed to get ready to chase down the woman. She was a deadly threat. One who could answer a lot of their questions.

"Don't leave me!"

Every muscle that had been ready to spring to action hardened. Jonathan turned back to Kate. She held Greg's hand in hers while the other rested under the side of his face against the asphalt. She wasn't crying, but the way her beautiful dark eyes reached out to him let him know that she was close. "Please, stay with me."

It was in that moment that he knew there was no other place he wanted to be.

He pulled out his phone and took a picture of the driver booking it away from the crime scene. A few bystanders were giving chase while he spotted a couple of drivers who had been waiting in line doing the same thing he was doing, taking quick pictures that would hopefully lead to an arrest once she was caught. With this many people eager to find her, Jonathan doubted her escape would be easy.

"It was the woman who followed us yesterday," Kate said as Jonathan crouched next to her. He nodded and watched as anger flashed across her face. When she looked down at Greg, it seemed to dissolve a bit. "He's breathing. I'm afraid to move him, though."

On a reflex he didn't know he had, Jonathan put his hand against her cheek, cradling it softly. Slowly she dragged her dark eyes up to his. The smile that graced her lips for only a second was small.

And then it was gone.

"It'll be okay," he said. "I promise."

Sirens could be heard in the distance. The crying and yelling still sounded around them. The woman and those chasing her were out of sight. Someone had turned off the car, but its exhaust created a nauseating smell in the air. Jonathan kept looking into Kate's eyes as she held a man she cared about deeply, praying he'd be okay.

For the first time since the accident, he realized the silver case hadn't left Kate's side. She'd kept it with her through it all.

What was in it?

And why was it worth killing for?

THE POLICE ARRIVED FIRST, then the ambulances. Jonathan, along with two others who had witnessed the entire thing, gave their statements first while EMTs rounded up those who were badly hurt.

Kate didn't leave Greg's side until the EMTs came for him. She quickly recalled his medical history and her fear that he had internal bleeding as they wheeled him to the vehicle. When they asked if she'd be riding with him, however, she said no.

"I've already called a close friend of his," she said. "He'll make it to the hospital before you will."

Kate clutched the silver case while she watched the ambulance take off. Jonathan was shocked she had declined riding with him, but before he could ask her reasoning, an EMT caught her attention.

"Miss, you're bleeding." The young man motioned

to the back of Kate's head. It prompted her to look down at her hand, where the blood from a little while ago had dried.

"It's just a superficial wound from hitting the asphalt," she said, dismissively. The EMT wasn't having any of it.

"Can I have a look?"

"It's fine."

The EMT smirked.

"Then you won't mind me having a quick look if it's no problem."

Jonathan couldn't help but mimic the man's smile. He got her there.

"Fine," she huffed. "Let's get this over with."

They followed the EMT back to an empty ambulance, where Kate perched on the lip of the vehicle. Jonathan was able to get a good look at her as she waited while the man did a quick examination.

The white blouse she wore was covered in dirt and grime, as were her navy dress pants. He even spied a tiny hole in the knee of one leg where she'd been resting on the ground next to Greg. Along with the blood on the back of her head, there was a patch of rubbed-off skin on her elbow where she'd hit the ground trying to get away from the car. Her hair was ruffled while her bangs had a gap in them where she'd rubbed her forehead due to the stress of everything. Her cheeks were tinted and her lips were still red, but her eyes had changed. While they had been playful during their talk with Greg in the coffee shop, now they were sharp. And angry. Not at the EMT poking at her head or Jonathan for hovering, but at the cause of what had happened.

The woman who had driven the car.

The man who left the bloody letter.

The same two he had suspected of following them the day before.

"Ow," Kate exclaimed, turning back at the EMT. "Watch it," she warned. Okay, so maybe she did have some anger for the man.

"Sorry," he muttered. "The cut isn't that bad back here. You don't need stitches, but it will be sore for a while. And, I'll state the obvious, you probably have a concussion and should go to the hospital to get it checked out."

The EMT stood back and swept his hand out to show he meant she should ride with him to the hospital. Kate didn't care. She got down and flashed him an apologetic smile.

"I'll be fine," she insisted. "Thanks for the concern."

The EMT looked to Jonathan.

"Are you sure, Kate?" he asked.

Kate nodded.

"When I was in college, I got into a car accident and had a bad concussion." She pointed to her head. "While I have a headache, this isn't bad. I just want to go back to the hotel now."

Jonathan wanted to push more, but he couldn't make her go to the ER. He looked back to the EMT.

"Sorry, man, but thanks for checking her out."

The young man shrugged and went back out into the

still-lingering crowd. Jonathan and Kate finally made it back to the sidewalk in front of the coffee shop. As they started their trek back, a coroner's van split the crowd in the street.

They paused in a moment of silence.

"This shouldn't have happened," Kate whispered when they started walking again. Jonathan kept his body between hers and the street. She kept the case between the two of them. He wondered if she'd let it go even once since leaving the coffee shop. "I just don't understand," she added. "I mean, if that's the same woman, then surely this all can't be a coincidence. Did you tell the cops about her and the man from the hotel?"

Jonathan nodded.

"He said, as of right then, they believed it to be an accident and the driver fled because she was either under the influence of something illegal or sheer fear and embarrassment of losing control of the car. But he would take down what I had to say and look into it." Jonathan was hiding his frustration. No matter how immense it was. Kate had already been through enough. He didn't need to escalate her nerves by adding his own. Still, she reacted badly to the news.

"An accident?" she squawked, attracting attention from the people walking around them. She didn't lower her voice. "She had an entire intersection to hit the brakes. Heck, after she killed those first two people by *running them over*, she could have put her foot on the brake pedal. No, what she did, she did on purpose. Greg is on his way to the hospital because that woman knew exactly what she was doing." Her free hand had fisted and her breathing had quickened. The passion she had exhibited when talking about the convention that morning was back. With a healthy dose of anger mixed in. She shook the case in her hand. "This is supposed to save people, not hurt them."

They were a block from the hotel. Jonathan looked away from Kate and kept his eyes peeled for any suspicious activity. He didn't comment on what she said until they finally made it to the hotel's elevator. When it closed them in, he turned and asked a question he'd been wanting to ask for a while.

"Normally Orion agents don't have to get too specific on client details," he started. "We give you the privacy you deserve. That is, until whatever information you're withholding puts you in danger. I'm not saying that woman was targeting you, or trying to scare you, or if she was desperate to get her hands on that silver case. However, if any of that is true, then I have to ask you one question." Jonathan grabbed her chin in his hand and tilted her eyes up until they were locked with his. "Kate, what's in the case?"

Chapter Eleven

The elevator beeped at their floor before Kate let out a breath. Jonathan held her face in his hand, but it was his eyes that once again had all of her attention. The fact that she could see every swirl of blue, a dark pond as still and beautiful as a painting, only highlighted the realization that the bodyguard was less than a few inches away from her lips.

Did he feel the urge to kiss her?

Did *she* feel the urge to kiss *him*?

No, Kate, she thought. *He wants to know what's in the case, that's all.*

"You saved my life, Jonathan," she stated, hedging around a response. "Thank you."

The bodyguard didn't want to relent—she could tell by the way he stayed still, not budging physically—but then the elevator doors started to close again. He stuck his hand out to stop them, turning away from her and letting her face go in the process. She felt the warmth of his skin even after the contact was broken.

"Are you sure you're okay?" Jonathan asked as they

walked toward their doors. She was thankful he'd dropped his earlier question but knew it was a matter of time before he'd ask again. If she was him, she would have kept nagging. Then again, Jonathan didn't seem like the type of person who nagged. "Yes, just a headache." She got her key card out and paused. "I didn't want to take this into the hospital," she said, motioning to the case in her hand. "But I would like to go there to check on Greg. Even though it's also not on the itinerary."

Jonathan's expression softened.

"That's no problem. I'd like to check on him, too."

Kate smiled a genuine smile at the man tasked with protecting her.

"Let me rinse off and then we can go."

They parted ways. Kate threw the top latch when her door was shut and took a moment to stare at it.

You aren't in any danger, she remembered thinking the day before. Thinking Jonathan's overprotectiveness had led to paranoia that had started to leak into her.

It's just in his head.

But now, could she claim the same?

The sound the car had made as it slammed into the first man and woman replayed in her head. She would have stayed frozen to the spot, terrified and unable to move, and been hit head-on had Jonathan not acted quickly. Sure, she'd hit her head in the process, but he'd saved her life by getting her out of the car's path. In that moment he'd truly done his job as bodyguard.

Greg's motionless body, crumpled against the asphalt, slid into her mind. The terror and anguish she'd first felt at seeing him started to grow within her again.

Had the woman really done that to him—to the rest of those walking over the crosswalk—because of Kate?

Her thoughts turned rapid, firing off in quick succession as she went through her interactions with her mentor in the last two decades. They went back as far as to include her mother in some.

I can't be the reason why he's hurt, she thought, moving back from the door like it had suddenly caught fire. *I just can't be.*

She turned her thoughts to the case in her hand and decided to slide it under the bed. Right then she needed to rinse the dirt and blood off her and head to the hospital. Until that morning she hadn't even known if she would get Greg's gift before the convention. She could wait another few hours before opening it.

A sigh escaped her lips as she stepped into the hot shower a minute later. Its temperature was instantly welcomed as each stream began to unknot the tension in her body. Trying to forget about how five years of her life were now being outshone by the last twenty-four hours in New York City was difficult to comprehend. Able to sidestep the violent, life-threatening parts, her thoughts turned to the man next door.

She ran her hands up and over her face, comparing Jonathan to herself. Before their talk with Greg she'd believed him to be as single-minded as she was about his work. But then he'd admitted he wanted roots.

Roots. Family. Love.

Could she claim the same? For the last five years and, to some extent, before she'd even begun her research, her life had revolved around the pursuit to save others from dealing with the same tragedy she had. She'd kissed, liked, dated and even shared her bed with a few suitors, but none of them had had staying power. They'd mistaken her unyielding determination for obsession instead of passion.

Kate paused to watch some of her blood swirl down the drain.

Had she blurred the line between the two?

Had her dream to prevent the senseless loss of life had the exact opposite effect on hers?

Pain exploded, hot and electric, on the back of her neck. Kate slapped at it, but by the time her hand touched the spot, the pain was gone. Confused, she ran her finger across the skin. The shock of pain didn't come back, but she realized there was a dull soreness radiating downward.

"What the—"

Kneading the skin around the source of the pain, she ran across a patch of skin that was raised. The dull soreness began to burn as it made its way down her body.

"Oh, my God."

Her thoughts began to race, her heart rate accelerating. She knew what this was. What solace or calm she'd tried to get from the hot shower definitely wasn't going to be obtained anymore. Turning off the water on reflex alone, she stumbled out of the shower and tried to take a breath.

It came out easily enough. Perhaps too easily. It turned into an extended yawn. Though the shower had woken her up considerably, Kate found her eyelids were growing heavy.

Too heavy.

Too fast.

Concern and confusion turned to fear as the feeling of wariness intensified.

Kate fumbled for a towel but missed it altogether. Her mind was trying to work overtime to make a plan of action while a haze was growing rapidly around her. She fumbled for her phone next to the sink. One thought was still bright enough to see among the enclosing fog. She quickly cycled through the names in her contacts before landing on one.

Quickly her fingers flew across the tiny keyboard while her vision began to blur. Her fear doubled, but it was just a thought. One her body wasn't responding to anymore. She hit Send, but her vision was spotting. She couldn't see if she'd hit the right button.

That worry alone propelled her out of the bathroom and to the adjoining door between her room and Jonathan's. She hoped the text had gone through. The way she was struggling to keep her eyes open made her doubt she'd have enough time to tell him what he needed to know.

The card to open the door was still on the TV stand. Kate dragged her palm against its top, trying to grab it. She was able to curl her fingers around the plastic, but when she turned back to the door, her legs buckled beneath her. The card fell along with her body until she was on all fours, struggling to manage a last-ditch knock.

However, the weight of unconsciousness was too much. It crushed her before she could even try to think of another plan.

And then Kate was naked, wet and alone.

"WHAT?"

Jonathan looked at his phone with his head cocked to the side and eyebrow raised. He hadn't expected and didn't understand the text on his phone from Kate.

Call jake not 922!!!

Jake? Nine hundred and twenty-two?

"What?" he asked the room again. His eyes traveled to the wall that separated their rooms just as his brain made sense of the random text. *Nine-one-one!*

Jonathan's body went on alert. He went to the adjoining door and knocked.

"Kate?"

He didn't hesitate.

Grabbing the key card, he unlocked the door and pushed it outward, but something kept it from swinging all the way open. He moved around the door and looked down to see what was blocking it. The scene he was met with was just as confusing as the text had been.

"Kate!"

She was lying on her side, slumped over on the ground, the door hitting her right shoulder. Her hand was out but empty, the card for the door discarded next to it. Like she had been trying to get to him but couldn't. Not only was she unconscious, she was also naked.

Jonathan didn't immediately check her. He had his fists up, ready to attack the man or woman who was behind her current state of distress. There was no one in the main room or bathroom. All he found was a bathroom filled with steam and a wet, naked woman against the carpet.

Then what had happened? Had her head injury caused this? But what was this?

"Kate," he said, urgency clear in his voice. Its tone or volume didn't stir the woman. Jonathan dropped to his knee and inspected her closer.

She had a pulse. It beat to a rhythm that wasn't strong but also wasn't weak. It thumped against his fingers on her neck with a steady beat that inspired an outpouring of relief on his end. He moved his attention to her chest, mindful not to focus on the more intimate parts, to find her breath pushing her body up and down with no apparent difficulty. Jonathan's eyes traveled the rest of her body, once again not with a focus that crossed the line between bodyguard and client, and couldn't find any identifying marks that suggested she'd been physically attacked.

"Kate?" he asked again. Moving her hair across her

cheek and away from her face, Jonathan saw a woman who looked almost peaceful.

Jonathan started to grab his phone—clearly Kate wasn't waking up—when he remembered the text.

Call jake not 922!!!

He had no doubt in his mind that she'd meant to say, "Nine-one-one," which meant she'd known something was about to happen to her. But why not call the one service you were supposed to call in a situation like this?

He cast a quick glance at the still brunette. He also had no doubt that the woman was smart, brilliant even. So it was no stretch of the imagination that Kathryn Spears knew more than he did about her current condition.

Jonathan just hoped this Jake person did, too.

Kate's phone was on the bathroom sink, still on the screen with the text she'd sent. Under different circumstances, he would have either been annoyed or amused to find his contact listed under the name *Mr. Bodyguard*. Instead he didn't have time to dawdle. He scrolled through her contacts to the one and only Jake. He hit Call without hesitating.

It rang twice.

"Kate?" a man answered, sounding surprised. "Can I call you back in two seconds?" A flurry of voices sounded on his end.

"This isn't Kate, and we need to talk *now*."

Jonathan might not have known anything about the man, but he could tell what had been surprise at getting Kate's call had tripled. With added aggression.

"Who is this? Where is Kate?" the man asked, audibly moving away from the voices in the background.

"My name is Jonathan Carmichael, I'm—"

"The bodyguard?"

That gave Jonathan pause.

"Yes," he admitted.

"What's wrong with Kate?" While Jake had been ready to go on the offensive with Jonathan, his tone had changed to one of acute concern. A whiplash effect that spoke volumes about him. Whoever the man was, he cared about Kate.

"Honestly, I don't know," Jonathan answered. "She sent me a text that said to call you and not nine-one-one. Less than a minute later I found her passed out on her hotel room floor." Jonathan didn't know why, but he left out the part about her being naked. Whether it was a weird jealousy he felt or a wild notion that he was somehow protecting her virtue, he had no idea. "She's breathing fine and has a normal pulse, but she's unresponsive. Less than an hour ago she got a concussion but said she knew it was fine."

The sound of a beep, maybe an elevator, Jonathan thought, popped in the background. Wherever Jake was, he was moving.

"No. If Kate said to call me and not an ambulance, then I can guarantee you she didn't pass out from a concussion. Have you called or told anyone about her?" he asked.

"No," Jonathan admitted, wondering for a second if he *had* made a mistake by calling Jake. "But since telling me to only call you was probably the last thing she did before she lost consciousness, I figured that was the best route to take."

"Good, that's good." Another faint beep traveled through the connection. "Has anyone come into contact with her in the last half hour?"

"Like I said, she was in an accident where she hit her head against the road."

"No, I mean, did anyone have physical, skin-to-skin contact with her?" Jake's frustration put Jonathan on edge. Instead of combating the feeling and the man it came from, it made him focus on the question.

"Aside from me and an unconscious work associate of hers, no." Then he remembered something. "Actually, an EMT checked her head in the back of an ambulance. Less than a half hour ago." As he said it, Jonathan knelt back down beside Kate. He put the cell phone between his shoulder and cheek to free up his hands. Gingerly, he ran his hands over the back of her hair, trying to find the wound. He found it and the dried blood over it.

"Check the back of her neck for any raised skin or mark," Jake rushed to say.

"Already ahead of you," Jonathan muttered, running his fingers down from the wound to the skin of her neck. Kate's skin was warm, wet and soft. "Wait."

Jonathan paused as his finger ran over a small bump on the back of her neck. He moved her hair out of the way and leaned closer, narrowing his eyes at the raised skin. "There's a bump in the middle of her neck. It isn't red or pink. I would have missed it had I not been feeling for it. There's also a tiny hole in the middle of it." Jonathan looked back into the bathroom. Aside from her clothes, there was nothing out of the ordinary as far as he could tell. "Did she do that to herself?"

"If she did, she's crazier than I thought," Jake said. "No, I think that EMT wasn't your run-of-the-mill paramedic."

"What?" Jonathan felt his muscles tense again. Getting warm, ready to attack. "Why would he do that?"

He looked down at Kate's relaxed face.

"I can only make a few guesses, and that would take up time we don't have." The warning behind Jake's words amplified the urgency Jonathan had carried moments before. "Text me the hotel address and room number. I need to make some calls on the way over there."

Jonathan's instinct to protect the privacy of his client flared to life.

"What's going on? Is she going to be okay?"

"No. Not if you play hardball with me," he spit out. "If you make me go through the trouble of tracing this call, we're going to lose minutes that could save her."

"Listen, buddy, I don't even know who you are," Jonathan pointed out.

Jake let out an aggravated sigh of frustration, barely dimmed by the sound of a car door shutting.

"You don't know me, but Kate does," he said. "She wanted you to call me and not the authorities because I know why she's in New York. I can't imagine she even told you that last part, did she?"

"The convention—" Jonathan started. The man was quick to interrupt.

"Is only the tip of the iceberg."

Chapter Twelve

Jonathan carefully picked up Kate's naked body and moved her to the bed. In any other situation, that alone would have been exhilarating in its own right. Taking a beautiful woman to bed without a stitch of clothing on her body would be followed by him joining her, also sans clothes.

However, Jonathan wasn't aroused in the least.

Instead, he was close to overwhelmed with concern.

"Don't worry, Kate," Jonathan whispered as he pulled the sheets and blanket up to her shoulders. "I'm going to fix this. Whatever this is."

Kate remained as unresponsive as she had been when he'd first found her. A fleeting thought that he should dress her crossed his mind, but he batted it away, afraid that jostling her too much might worsen her condition.

Not that he knew what her condition was, except that someone had injected her with something that had left her unconscious.

He looked once again at her relaxed face—peaceful—

and was bowled over by how beautiful she was. The concern he felt for her future ran deep. How had a woman he'd only known for two days gotten so far beneath his skin? Was that even possible?

He watched as the sheets moved up and down as she breathed softly.

Yes, somehow it was possible.

Jonathan didn't leave her side until a knock sounded on the door to his room. He gave her one more quick look before going through the adjoining room—shutting the door behind him—and heading to answer the knock. His body was tense, like a snake readying to strike at the first sign of a threat. He peered through the peephole to see a man standing by himself.

Jonathan pushed aside the lingering fear that he had made a huge mistake in listening to Kate's text and opened the door.

Jonathan placed Jake around the same age as him. He was shorter, around six feet, but lean just like him. Jonathan bet the black blazer that matched his slacks hid toned muscles that worked in tandem with a trained posture. Beneath the blazer was a white button-up and a black-and-dark-blue-striped tie. The outfit was finished off with dress shoes that almost reflected the hallway lights. His hair was also neat, dark blond and cropped short, while his face was cleanly shaven. Even his eyes, a pale blue, seemed to be proper. Jonathan would bet money this guy was some type of law enforcement. Then again, that didn't mean Jonathan trusted him any more in the moment.

"Where is she?" the man greeted, body already angling like he had been invited inside. Even though he didn't introduce himself, his voice matched the one on the phone. But Jonathan had to be sure he could trust him before allowing him anywhere near Kate.

"How do I even know if you're here to help?" Jonathan asked, voice as cold as steel.

The man didn't hide his frustration. It turned his expression into a scowl.

"You don't," he admitted. "But I swear to you if Kate dies while you're out here trying to be a good bodyguard, then wouldn't that be a kick in the professional ass?"

There was no humor in his words, just sincerity.

It was that sureness that made Jonathan turn around, key card already in hand for the adjoining door.

"If you do *anything* I think is hurting her, I'll kill you," Jonathan growled.

The man followed him into the room.

"I thought bodyguards protected, not killed."

"I'd make the exception for her."

Jake didn't respond as they moved to the other room.

"I moved her off the floor," Jonathan said, pointing out the obvious just in case it affected whatever magic Jake was supposed to generate to fix the situation. "She had just gotten out of the shower."

Jake went over to Kate so fast that Jonathan fisted his hands. He kept the man's pace and watched as he bent over her.

"Careful," Jonathan warned. Jake didn't pause in

his actions. He turned her head carefully to the side to look at the mark on her neck himself. It lasted less than a second.

"This paramedic looked her over after the car ran Greg down?" he asked, attention falling away from Kate.

"Yes," Jonathan answered, surprised. "How did you know about the accident?"

Jake pointed his thumb back at Kate.

"She called me after it happened." Jonathan connected the dots. So Jake had been the close friend Kate had called to go to the hospital when she couldn't. That eased some of Jonathan's suspicion of the man. But only some. "I'm working on a project with Greg here in New York," he added, as if that explained anything, but Jonathan was only concerned about one thing.

"So what's wrong with Kate?"

For the first time since the man had walked through the door, he looked Jonathan straight in the eyes.

"How seriously do you take your job as her bodyguard?"

Jonathan squared his shoulders.

"Very."

"Then we need to leave *now*." Jake was already walking away, head lowered in an obvious show of determination. But, once again, nothing was being explained.

"Wait, leave?"

Jake turned quick, angry.

"Listen here—" he started, but Jonathan had had

enough. He pushed the man until his back slammed into the wall. He didn't stop there, lifting him slightly by the collar of his shirt.

"No, you listen here," Jonathan fumed. "I don't know you, I don't even know your last name and I don't know where it is you expect me to go. But I'll tell you right now, I'm not one of those people who run on pure faith alone. I need some answers."

Jonathan's adrenaline was pumping through his veins. He could have done some serious damage to the man—shown him exactly how physical suspicion could be—but Jonathan was letting one fact and one fact alone hold his anger back.

Kate had asked him to call the man.

Jake appeared to be wrangling his own knee-jerk reactions. When he spoke there was a sharp edge to his words.

"My name is Jake Harper and I'm a federal agent. My badge is in my blazer pocket, right side," he explained. Jonathan lowered the man back to the ground and motioned for him to show said badge. He pulled out the black flip wallet and, just as he said, Jake Harper, FBI, was on it. "I've known Kate since she was eight, and I've worked with Greg for the last five years."

"You know what she was injected with," Jonathan stated.

Jake nodded.

"I wouldn't have, had she gone to the hospital, but if she truly asked you to call me instead, then she must know I can help. And there's only one thing I would even guess could make her drop like that." He put his badge back into his pocket. Jonathan caught a glimpse of the holstered gun beneath his jacket. "If I'm right, and there's a good chance I am, then we need to give her another specific injection from Greg's lab."

"And if we don't?" Jonathan was almost afraid to ask.

"Then she dies." Jake didn't pause to let that sink in. "So, bodyguard, you said you were willing to kill for her. Now the question is, are you willing to help steal for her?"

IT WAS RAINING.

The pitter-patter of drops hitting the tin roof was an ocean of sound around her, filling the tiny bedroom with comforting white noise. The soft glow of her bedside lamp projected hundreds of tiny stars on the ceiling. She looked up at them from where she'd fallen asleep on the rug and drew a line in the air connecting a cluster, creating Orion's belt with ease. She'd never been able to spot the constellation before, but now she was sure of how its placement looked. It made her happy, though she couldn't figure out why.

The rain got harder and tore her attention away. She heard a distant slam followed by voices. Quickly, she jumped up and crawled into bed. She wasn't supposed to be awake.

The rain got even harder and the stars went out, bathing everything in darkness. Something was wrong. Fear twisted around her heart at the sound of footsteps in the hallway. They weren't heavy like a man's, but softer. Excitement banished all fear. The star lights flashed back on and even the rain quieted as the door to the bedroom cracked open. A woman's face appeared in the space, searching for her.

"Kate, aren't you supposed to be asleep?"

Kate giggled.

"Mom, I was waiting for you," she said matter-of-factly. "You were gone for a long time!"

Cassandra opened the door wide, already kicking off her boots and throwing her jacket to the floor. She came up to the bed and said, "Scoot!"

Kate did as she was told and soon they were both squeezed into the twin-size bed. Kate didn't mind one bit.

"I told you not to wait up for me," Cassandra said, putting her arm around Kate and smooshing her into her side. "You have your first day of third grade tomorrow. You're going to be tired." Cassandra tickled her side a few times until Kate laughed.

The sound became so loud it blocked out all other noises. The stars flickered. A wave of cold wrapped around Kate.

"Don't be scared," Cassandra whispered.

And then everything felt right in the room.

"I'm not scared," Kate said, pouting. She didn't want her mother to think she wasn't strong. She slid her hand down to the badge on her belt and ran her finger over the gold. She'd always loved tracing the three letters with her fingertips.

Cassandra kissed the top of Kate's head.

"Just because someone's scared doesn't mean they aren't strong."

Kate felt her cheeks heat, embarrassed that she'd had to be taught a lesson and hadn't learned it on her own.

"Jake says *he's* not afraid of anything, because his dad gave him a badge like his to carry around," Kate said. Cassandra laughed, but the sound was off. Like being underwater. Kate tilted her head up to see what the cause was. Cassandra's eyes were closed, lips turned downward like she was sleeping.

"Mom?" Kate whispered.

Cassandra didn't move.

"Is that what you want? A badge?" she asked, and though her lips still didn't move, Kate knew it was her mother asking. Her voice filled the small room like it was coming through a school intercom. She felt a finger press lightly against her temple. It was cold. "Because I believe *this* is your greatest weapon, and you should, too. You're smart and clever and the world will quake beneath your feet if you ever decide to conquer it."

The frozen Cassandra thawed in a fit of laughter. Kate joined in, liking the way the sounds harmonized.

"If I ruled the world, I'd make everyone have brownies for dinner," Kate said. "And bedtime would be whenever I wanted."

"That's my girl."

She looked up to see if her mother really did approve, but Cassandra was gone. Kate scrambled out of bed, trying to escape the growing feeling that something terrible had happened. Something was horribly wrong. She ran through the doorway, with her parents' room in mind, when suddenly she was no longer in her house.

Where she was now smelled old and weird. Half of it Kate could process, the other half she didn't understand. It was dark, too.

Someone tugged at her hand.

She turned her head to see them.

"Kate?"

Jonathan was staring back at her, blue eyes nearly lost in the darkness around them.

"Where's Jake?" she asked, unease building into panic. "We rode our bikes here."

Jonathan didn't seem to care. Instead he looked over her head, focusing on something with interest. Kate turned and saw what caught his eye. A figure in the distance, sitting in an open room all alone.

"We shouldn't go in there," Jake's voice whispered now at her side. There was real fear in it. Fear that coursed through their hands held together. "We need to go get help."

"Just because we're scared doesn't mean we aren't strong," Kate chanted. She started forward, slowly moving closer to the person in the chair.

Kate heard Jake follow—heard his footsteps echo in the abandoned building—and felt braver. She could be strong just like her mom. She could find out who the person was. She could help them.

The closer she came, though, the farther away she ended up. The never-ending hallway became darker and darker until the old building, Jake and the person in the chair disappeared altogether.

"Don't worry, Kate," Jonathan's voice said, now the only thing around her. "I'm going to fix this."

One by one the stars on the ceiling turned back on. Kate was back in her bedroom, but this time it was different. Sitting on the rug, tears in her eyes, was a little girl dressed in black. Between her small hands was a shiny gold badge.

Jonathan's words continued to echo around the two of them. They were strong and powerful, but Kate knew they were just words.

"You can't fix this," she whispered. "No one can."

Chapter Thirteen

Jake blew through a red light, swerving around a car driving past the intersection. Jonathan gripped the handle of the passenger door. He wasn't afraid, but he couldn't deny that he was anxious. He'd just met the man ten minutes ago and now they were speeding toward an apparently secret lab for an equally secret antidote.

It was all very James Bond.

"I know you have no good reason to trust me, but I'm afraid you're going to have to," Jake reiterated. "After we get what we need and administer it to Kate, I'll let her explain everything she's willing to—she can do that better than I can, at least—and everything will make more sense."

Jonathan was starting to doubt anyone had all the answers to connect the dots that had sprung up in the last two days, but he was willing to hold out hope.

"Are you at least going to give me more info on this 'secret lab' of yours?" he asked, making finger quotes around the part that undoubtedly made it sound like he was in a spy movie. "Is it a part of the FBI?"

A car horn blared at their side as Jake did some more defensive driving. Instead of hitting the brakes, he smoothly dipped into oncoming traffic before swerving back to the original lane, passing the taxi that had thought it a good idea to cut them off.

"Yes and no," Jake answered, unaffected by the high speeds and subsequently more dangerous obstacles in their way. It made Jonathan think he'd done it before. "The lab was created and is currently funded and maintained by the FBI, but only a few know about it. The facility is run by its lead scientist, Greg Calhoun."

"He said he was in business consulting now, only dabbling in scientific pursuits," Jonathan interrupted, paraphrasing what the man had said earlier.

Jake snorted.

"He lied," he said. "And before you get your panties all in a twist about being lied to, you must understand that even Kate doesn't know about his involvement with the FBI or, for that matter, that Greg in no form or fashion lives or works in Buffalo. He's never even been to Buffalo. Hell, she doesn't even know of my involvement with Greg."

"Which is what?"

Jake cast him a look that perfectly exhibited pride and simultaneous defeat.

"I'm his handler." The defeat—the guilt—now made sense. "Normally I wouldn't have been assigned a job like this—it was given to me barely out of the academy—but Greg said the only way he'd agree to work with the Bureau was if he could pick who oversaw his work and the day-to-day operations. He picked me."

"You grew up with Kate," Jonathan added, realizing the connection. "That means you—"

"Also grew up with Greg around," Jake finished. "That's why he chose *me*. He trusted me, and now—" Jake cut himself off by slamming his hands against the SUV's steering wheel. "He's in the hospital, and now Kate?" He quieted a moment but didn't give Jonathan enough time to say anything before he spoke again. "The power went off in my building last night and killed my alarm clock. I'm not one of those people who can just wake up to the sound of their phone. I need both. Without the first, I woke up late and missed a call from Greg saying he was going to meet Kate. I was supposed to go with him. I was supposed to be there. I was supposed to protect him." Again, Jake's anger at fate, or himself, boiled over. He punched the steering wheel. Normally Jonathan would have stopped the rant. He didn't know Jake, so how could he relate to him?

But, the thing was, he absolutely could.

In a way Jake was Greg's bodyguard, just with a different title. He was responsible for keeping him safe. For protecting someone he cared about. As soon as that car had floored it through that intersection, he had failed.

Just as Jonathan had with Kate.

Empathy started to create a fondness for Jake, but that didn't mean it would last. There were still too many questions he needed answered first.

"So what does Greg have to do with what happened to Kate? And why are the injections we need in his lab?" he asked, trying to grasp *something*.

While Jake had admitted freely that there was a secret lab and he was Greg's handler, these questions made him hesitate. "Listen, if I'm about to help you *steal* from a lab operated by the *Federal Bureau of Investigation*, then you're going to tell me why."

Jake turned on his blinker seconds before taking a quick turn. Another series of car horns went off. So far the traffic hadn't been too bad, a fact that made Jonathan again realize Jake had done this before. When they were heading straight again, he let out a long breath.

"Kate has been working on the beginnings of a drug that could help law enforcement in a phenomenally big way. One that could help turn the tides on interrogation while remaining one hundred percent humane," he explained. "She brought the idea to Greg, who was an FBI consultant at the time. To his surprise, it actually seemed plausible. He pitched the idea to an FBI task force dealing with scientific pursuits. Instead of simply taking the idea for themselves, Greg convinced them that Kate's singular focus and passion for the project would benefit them more than a bunch of old scientists trying to become famous. I guess they agreed, but only in part. They let Greg find funding and contacts for her to start her research while giving Greg the same tools. He was told to oversee her work while simultaneously trying to work on it alongside her. While some believed in Greg's vote of confidence for Kate, others thought she was too young, too inexperienced, to come up with any usable end goal, especially before they could." The FBI agent cut Jonathan a quick smile. "But she did."

"She doesn't know about Greg working on the same thing then, does she?" Jake shook his head. "So what was supposed to happen when she finished?" He didn't understand how the convention fit into the picture. Jake seemed to pick up on that thread of thought.

"The convention is a somewhat private event where scientific and technological inventions and ideas are presented to potential investors to try to get more funding. It's also a way to monitor possible future security threats—shutting down could-be mad scientists," he added with a tone that said he was joking, though Jonathan was sure he wasn't. "I think the idea was to get her to the convention, have her make her case and then offer her a job. Then let her know what Greg had been up to."

"And if she didn't take the job? What was the plan then?"

"They would have continued her work and made all attempts to keep her from receiving any other funding. Until she'd have to accept." At least Jake didn't sound happy about that plan. "And before you ask, yes, she would have eventually accepted. Kate might not have gone the exact route I did, but she's always wanted to be part of the FBI. It's just in our blood."

Before Jonathan could ask what he meant by that, another flurry of questions came to mind.

"So what the hell was she injected with? The drug

she created? And how did she know to call you if she didn't even know about Greg's laboratory here?"

Jake's jaw tightened.

"Kate is a very cautious person. Up until now she hasn't started testing on her finished product—that's what the next step is supposed to be. However, Greg isn't as cautious. He synthesized a version of it off her current notes and gave it to her as a present during a visit, a memento of all the work she'd done so far."

"She took it," Jonathan guessed, already picking up on his hardened body language.

"Yes. Frustration got the better of her. It was too early in the research stages and the effects were dangerous. If Greg hadn't been there to counteract them... Well, let's just say you wouldn't be in New York right now." For the first time since Jonathan had gotten into the SUV, they began to slow. "He said he'd make a few more vials just in case someone ever accidentally did it again. Being his handler, I was also there with them. I suppose that's the only reason Kate wanted you to call me."

"She knew you would put it together."

"She doesn't know that I know the location of Greg's lab, but I'm guessing she assumed, being FBI, I'd have a good chance of figuring it out."

"That would also mean that she knew she was injected with the failed drug," Jonathan said. "A failed version of *her* drug. One that was made in an FBI-sanctioned lab..."

"Which means the couple you told me about when

we first got into the car had access to the lab and the failed samples Greg kept for further study."

"Or someone helped them get it."

"Let me worry about that later," Jake seethed, knuckles tightening around the steering wheel until they were white. "What we need to focus on now is stealing from a lab that isn't supposed to exist."

"Don't you have access, though?"

Jake shook his head.

"No one except Greg is allowed to take anything out of the lab. Even if I explained, they still wouldn't let me grab the injections and would most likely lock them down instead."

"So what do you need me to do?"

Jake took one last turn into a two-story parking garage. He flashed his badge at the parking attendant before he even had a chance to stand. The gate began to retract and Jake continued inside. He drove to the back corner and parked in a spot reserved for over-nighters. He cut the ignition and turned, a smirk clear as day on his face.

"I need you to be a distraction."

THE RAIN DIDN'T come back.

Kate instead only heard the sound of voices float-ing down the hallway to her bedroom. She didn't like the voices. They made her cold.

"Want to see it again?"

She turned to look at the boy next to her. He was playing with something in his hands.

"It's not a real badge, Jake," she answered. "It doesn't even say the right thing."

Jake didn't let her harsh words bother him. He shrugged.

"We need to get closer so I can hear," she declared.

"Kate, that isn't a good idea."

A man appeared in the corner, leaning against her dresser.

"I can't hear them," she insisted.

"You don't have to do this," he responded. He didn't blink as he spoke. The stars from her lamp now attached to his shirt.

"If I don't get closer, I won't know what they're talking about," she reasoned again, already getting up. She took Jake's hand and tugged him along after her into the hall. The voices got louder.

"If he's lying, then what?" her father asked. He sounded scared. It made her pause.

"You can go back to your room," Jonathan offered, now standing next to her. "You don't need to do this again, Kate. You can't change what happens."

Kate shook her head, trying to clear his voice out of her head.

"Deacon, they'll find them," the woman said.

A loud ringing exploded throughout the house. Kate threw her hands over her ears and tried to yell, but nothing came out.

Suddenly she was in the office. Jake had the house phone pressed against his ear, hand over the receiver.

Kate watched as he carefully hung up the phone and began to speak to someone else in the room.

It was a girl.

Both of their mouths moved, but no words came out. Kate could tell the two were excited. Afraid, but excited.

She followed them back to the girl's bedroom and watched as they opened the window.

"Don't go," Kate warned, though she couldn't remember why. Jake and the girl didn't listen and soon they were out of the window and running across the grass to their bikes.

"They're worried about their mom and dad," Jonathan said from his seat on the bed. "They're being brave."

Kate shook her head, the intensifying feeling of wrongness making her start to cry.

"They shouldn't go," she cried. "I shouldn't have gone."

Chapter Fourteen

He didn't like the plan.

Not one bit.

No matter that there was still a good chance that this was all some elaborate setup.

One giant lie that would only spell giant trouble for him.

"You ready?" Jake asked, holding the bag up.

Jonathan looked at it with annoyance.

"From what you've said, I don't think we even have time to go back over this very bad plan of yours."

Jake flipped the bag upside down.

"You're right," he said. Jake didn't hesitate putting the bag over Jonathan's head. The world instantly went dark.

Completely and utterly dark.

"Put your hands behind your back now."

Jonathan did as he was told, still in no form or fashion liking the plan. He felt a zip tie go around his wrists but, thankfully, it wasn't tightened all the way.

"Just in case," Jake said, voice lowered. "Now, let's

get to walking. And remember, no talking. If we're going to keep this under wraps, I don't need you to incriminate yourself."

Jonathan snorted.

A very, very bad plan.

Jake grabbed hold of his arm and together they began to walk away from the car.

"You know, I've got to hand it to you," Jake whispered. "To go through this, the risks you're taking, you're either really dedicated to your job or Kate's made quite the impression on you."

Jonathan let those words sink in. On the one hand, he was extremely dedicated to his job. When he succeeded, despite unforeseen obstacles, Orion Security Group succeeded. Which meant Nikki, Mark, Oliver and all of their loved ones succeeded, as well. It was a trickle-down effect that he'd always strived to keep positive.

On the other hand, Kate *had* made quite the impression on him. In less than two days, she had annoyed him, frustrated him, angered him and, yet, she'd also surprised him. Her passion—her drive—was so strong it was nearly tangible. Where others, like the ex she'd mentioned, had seen it as perhaps a flaw—an obstacle to getting to know her—Jonathan saw something else. He saw love and perseverance and patience. Kate was so focused on completing something meant to save lives that she'd practically given up her own to see it get done. She'd sacrificed herself for strangers. Sure, she'd been a pain in the backside to him, but Jonathan was starting to see that a woman like Kathryn Spears was much more than her snark. She had a good heart.

And that heart needed protecting.

So, without answering the man Jonathan believed to be Kate's closest friend, he walked in darkness, ready to accept whatever consequences might come his way.

"We're about to get in an elevator that will take us to the basement," Jake whispered after they'd walked for less than a minute. "This isn't the usual way in, so we'll be seen. Don't talk."

Jonathan nodded and soon the sounds of the outside world became muffled and then disappeared. He heard a series of clicks before the motion of moving downward pulled at his stomach. Jonathan half expected to be in the elevator for much longer than it took to get between one floor and the next, envisioning a secret lab much farther down, maybe even in an abandoned subway tunnel or the sewers, but the movement stopped after one floor.

The door slid open and a wave of cold air met them. Still, the bag blocked him from seeing his surroundings. Jonathan moved his wrist around slightly, making sure he could get out of the tie if need be. It silenced some of his nerves.

They walked straight off the elevator and took a sharp left. From there they continued straight for at least thirty seconds before taking a step down. Jake's grip on his arm tightened for a moment.

Jonathan rolled back his shoulders before pulling away from Jake's grip. The agent responded by tightening his grip again before pulling Jonathan forward with obvious aggression.

"If you don't stop fighting me, I'll break your kneecaps," Jake growled loudly. Jonathan continued to fight against him, but Jake had the upper hand. He shoved him forward until Jonathan finally heard the other man.

"What's this?" the third man asked. He was farther away, and soon after he spoke, the rollers of a chair scraped the ground. He'd been sitting.

"Someone who needs to be taught a lesson in manners," Jake said smartly, still struggling with Jonathan. "I need to ask him a few questions and this was the safest and closest place to do it."

"But no one is allowed down here since the lockdown," the guy said. "Sorry, but you'll have to take him somewhere else."

"Listen, you heard about what happened to Greg?"

There was a silence in which Jonathan guessed the guard nodded.

"I think this guy can help lead us to the people who were behind it." The man must not have looked convinced. "Listen, until we find out who did this, Greg is still in danger, and I'm not willing to let him die because of a traffic jam between here and the Bureau. Are you?"

For added effect, Jonathan chose that moment to break free of Jake's hold and lurch forward into the unknown. The men behind him reacted fast. Someone's full weight crashed into him and pinned him hard to the tile. The second man came up and together they lifted Jonathan back to his feet.

"Take him into the back room so he doesn't break anything in here," said the guard.

"Thanks, Barry," Jake replied, already moving Jonathan forward.

They walked for what felt like several hundred feet before the sound of a door opening and closing met his ears. Jake pushed Jonathan hard, causing him to stumble into what felt like a table.

"Sit down and don't move," he barked out.

Jonathan did as he was told, finding a chair with rollers. Once he was seated, Jake grabbed the chair's arms and pulled him away from the table to the middle of the room, apparently away from anything. Jonathan heard another chair's rollers scraping against the floor before it seemed to be positioned across from him.

"Barry is a good man, but he's very protective of Greg and the people who work here every day," Jake said. "The way he looked at me when I said you might know who is behind Greg's current condition... He may get physical with you, even though I'll tell him not to." And then he heard Jake stand and walk away. He called out to Barry without waiting for any kind of response from Jonathan. "I need you to watch him for a second. I need to take this call."

Barry didn't question or complain this time around. Jonathan heard his footfalls and then a quick exchange of whispered words between the two men. The sound of Jake talking louder came back. He was pretending to be on a call, getting him into the lab while their only obstacle, Barry, was in the same room with Jonathan.

This time the door wasn't shut.

Jonathan hoped Barry's focus would remain on him and not what Jake was doing in the other room.

KATE COULDN'T SEE ANYTHING, but she knew she was in a box. Just like she *knew* she was naked. Those were two facts that she accepted as absolute truth.

She ran her hands over the wood that enclosed her, trying to feel for a way out while also trying to determine why she was there at all. Then the inside of the box lit up.

She wasn't in just any box.

She was in a coffin.

Pain in the back of her neck moved an already terrified feeling to its limit. Tears sprang to her eyes as she threw her fists against the top. It did nothing to damage the wood.

"Help!" she yelled.

No one responded.

She pounded on the lid and its sides for what felt like an eternity, but nothing changed. The wood didn't splinter or crack, and no called out to her.

She was alone.

Unwilling to give up, she scooted as far to the side as she could to see where the light was coming from. Through eyes blurred by tears, she could just make out the shape of star lights against the wood.

"Kate?"

The sound of someone yelling above her made her focus back on the lid. Instead of relief pouring through her, a deep coldness enveloped her. It started against her back and slowly moved up across her skin. The light from the stars flickered. Kate turned her head to see why.

She screamed.

Water was seeping in through each star and rising at an alarming rate. It was already to her ears.

"Help!" she yelled again, resuming her pounding against the lid.

The water moved higher until she had to prop herself up on her elbows, trying to keep her head above water. However, the attempt seemed to make it rise faster. She turned her head, pressing her cheek to the wood, and took one last long breath seconds before the box was completely filled.

The flickering lights stabilized, continuing their earlier, steady glow. Kate wasn't only going to drown, she was going to be able to watch herself do it.

Pain in the back of her neck shot downward and dispersed.

She was going to die.

THE PUNCH PROBABLY didn't come out of nowhere. Had Jonathan been able to see, he would have picked up on the physical signs that Barry was about to clock him one good. He would have seen the tension in his arm, in his shoulder and in his jaw. All tightening as a result of acute anger or adrenaline or both. He would have

DO YOU WANT TO GET REWARDED WITH FREE BOOKS?

Join today.
It's fun, easy, and free...

*"I just wanted to tell you how happy I am with the rewards program you are now offering. I signed up a year ago and I already have redeemed **over 18 free books**. Thank you, Valerie"*

Don't miss out...
Join today and
earn a FREE book.*

also seen the expression, or complete lack of one, and realized that the man sitting across from him was indeed very protective of his colleagues.

The punch landed against the right side of Jonathan's jaw. It sent his head reeling to the left as pain exploded along the bone. Jonathan didn't know what Barry looked like, but from his voice alone he'd bet the man was similar in size to him. By the power behind his punch, Jonathan guessed the man had less muscle, though. A blessing given the current situation.

"Who hit him?" Barry asked, voice low so Jake couldn't hear. "Who is the woman who hit Mr. Calhoun?"

Jonathan snorted.

That's exactly what I'd like to know, too, Barry.

"Are you laughing? Is this *funny to you*?" Barry seethed. Jonathan braced for another hit. He turned his head to the other side, hoping to catch the new hit on a spot that wasn't already throbbing. But then he heard the man's chair push back. He was now standing in front of him. No matter where he decided to hit, Jonathan knew it was going to hurt.

A sound of glass shattering in the lab put a halt to Barry's wrath. Jonathan froze. If Barry got at all suspicious of Jake's intention, then Jake would have no choice but to keep him quiet.

"If there's a chance someone on the inside is involved with whatever is going on with Greg and Kate, then I want to find out on my own," Jake had said after they'd run through their plan in the parking garage.

"I'm sure Kate will tell you later why I have trust issues, but until I figure this out, I'm not going to trust anyone. That's why I couldn't do this by myself. I need to stay in the clear if I want to see this through."

Jonathan saw the same determination in Jake that Kate displayed about her work. The agent suspected someone had betrayed their task force—their team—and was going to do everything in his power to crack the mystery wide open.

But not if he got caught.

"Jake, what are you—" Barry started to ask. He didn't get the chance to finish the question. Jonathan rocked up on his feet and threw his shoulder into the man's chest so quickly that he didn't have time to dodge the attack. The two of them toppled over Barry's chair and once again Jonathan hit the ground hard, but not harder than Barry. He could hear the man's breath wheeze out and decided to use that against him. He slid one hand out of the tie binding his wrists together and struck out, connecting with the man's face. He made a grunt and then went limp.

Jonathan waited a moment.

Barry still didn't move.

Slowly, Jonathan rose to his feet and lifted the bottom of the bag. Barry was most definitely unconscious.

The sound of quick footsteps made him turn around just as Jake slid into the doorway. He looked at Jonathan and then down at Barry.

"It was either that or you would have been caught,"

Jonathan said, answering the unasked question. "Plus, you were right. He did get physical."

Jake let out a quick breath but nodded. In his hand was a small black bag.

"We need to leave."

Jonathan followed the man into the lab and paused. Workstations covered in machines, vials, papers and things Jonathan didn't recognize littered the room. He pictured Kate among them all, head bent over a microscope before going to one of the walls that was nothing but a whiteboard, concentrated yet just as excited. Imagining her working made him smile, but at the same time soured in his stomach. This was her element. Her life.

One he just didn't understand.

"Fast thinking, taking him down. I accidentally knocked over an empty vial," Jake said, running over to a small office in the corner next to the hall they had originally come down. "I'm going to reboot the security cameras. It should give us enough time to make it back to the car."

"Are there cameras in here?" Jonathan asked, following. Jake still had the bag in his hand.

"No, lab work isn't supposed to be monitored, just the exits."

"What about when Barry wakes up? Won't he realize you helped me?"

Jake's hands flew across the computer's keyboard.

"I wouldn't be leaving here with you if I didn't have a plan," he said when he had finished. "Now, run!"

Jonathan followed as Jake ran into the hallway. Unlike the lab it was narrow and cold, its walls a crumbling white that barely reflected the lights. They ran until they took a sharp right to the elevator. It wasn't as old or as high-tech as Jonathan had envisioned. It looked like a normal elevator with only two floors as options, disappointing his inner James Bond fan.

They didn't speak as Jake punched the two buttons in a quick five-figure sequence and the elevator began to ascend. Seconds later it dinged, opening up to the first floor of the parking garage. In the distance Jonathan could see the SUV.

"Your secret lab is under a parking garage," Jonathan said, sarcasm lacing his voice, as soon as they got into the vehicle. Jake started the engine and handed Jonathan the bag.

"Hey, until just now you didn't know it was here, so mission accomplished."

Jonathan had to agree with that.

"We should have brought Kate with us," Jonathan said. "We could have given this to her now."

Jake shook his head.

"I wasn't sure how this would shake out," he admitted. "Things could have gotten much more intense. I would have hated for Kate to get hurt while we're trying to save her."

Jake was right, but that didn't mean that Jonathan didn't feel the pressure of time against them. Kate had been unconscious for far too long for his liking. He looked down at the bag in his hands. It was small and not at all heavy.

"Are you sure this will save her?" he asked, back to serious.

Jake matched his tone.

"I sure hope so."

Chapter Fifteen

A fist broke through the coffin's lid just as Kate's body floated to the bottom. She focused on it, inches from her face, as cracks from the new hole spiderwebbed through the rest of the lid. Slowly, and then with startling speed, the water began to drain upward and out of the coffin.

Kate kept her focus on the fist, still balled, even as she coughed, gasping for air.

"Who are you?" she asked once she could breathe again.

The fist finally opened into a hand that reached out for her, beckoning her to take it. So she did.

It pulled her from the coffin with ease, shattering the lid and leaving the horrors behind. Its warmth guided her through a moment of darkness before she was standing, naked and wet, in a warehouse.

The warehouse.

Kate wanted to turn to see if her savior was behind her but couldn't move. All of her attention was at the end of a room in the distance. People were standing, backs to her, all looking at the person in the center.

The person hunched over in a chair.

Kate's feet slapped against the cold concrete, but didn't make a sound as she walked toward them. That room. That person. She couldn't remember what they had to do with her. Why she was there.

She needed to finally find out.

She needed to remember.

Kate stopped among the people gathered around the person in the middle. Even though she was so close, she couldn't make out who it was. However, the faces around her she had little trouble recognizing.

Jake, tall and in his FBI uniform, stood closest to her, eyes never leaving the person in the chair. Next to him was Greg, smiling like he always did, a silver case in his hand. Her father was there farther back. He was young and upset. She couldn't remember why.

"Kate, we shouldn't be here."

Able to finally turn around, she saw a little girl holding a little boy's hand. The girl didn't care about his warning. She looked through Kate at the woman in the chair.

The woman.

Terror and anguish collided in her chest as she remembered where she was.

When she was.

And who the woman was.

Kate turned and was suddenly kneeling in front of her.

"Mom?"

The rope around Cassandra was tied so tightly to

the chair that at first it appeared as if she was sitting up on her own. Her hair that she'd always worn back in a ponytail for work had fallen out of its holder and covered half of her face. The other half was covered in blood, still dripping. Her eye was swollen shut and there was duct tape across her mouth.

Kate stumbled backward just as the little girl walked forward. Her eyes were wide, glazed over. With shaking little hands, she reached for the tape and took it off.

"Mom?" she whispered.

The little boy started to put his arms around her when his focus caught on something in the corner.

"Dad?" he yelled, dropping her hand and running out of view.

Kate didn't watch—instead she looked back at the girl.

But she was gone and so was everyone else except for Cassandra.

"I found you," Kate whispered. "Dad thought the call was a fake, but we didn't listen and we found you first." Kate took an uncertain step forward. "You weren't breathing. I heard them tell Dad you'd been gone for hours. I tried to untie you," Kate continued, voice shaking, "but it was too hard. I wasn't strong enough."

She looked down at the ropes again, angry at them like she had been all those years ago. Suddenly, she felt the need to try again. Kate moved to the back of the chair and found the three knots. She tried to undo them, a feeling of defeat already rising, but the first one came undone. She paused, surprised, but then moved to the next one. It too came undone in her hands. She moved to the last one and, with a cry of joy, it unknotted.

Kate squeezed her eyes shut, trying to stop her tears.

"I did it," she said, voice wavering. "I finally untied them."

"Good job."

Her eyes flashed open and she was no longer standing. She was back in the coffin. However, this time, the lid was gone, open to a white ceiling. Panic started to seize her once more when the feeling of running water moved across her bare skin again. She began to flail around.

"Don't worry, I'm here," said a voice next to her. "Kate, I'm here."

It was Jonathan.

He held her against his chest while the water moved higher and higher.

"Don't worry, you're safe now," he said.

And Kate decided that was all she needed to hear.

KATE STOPPED STRUGGLING against him.

"I think she heard you," Jake said from next to the tub. "That means it's working."

Jonathan stroked Kate's hair away from her face as the cold water rained down on them both from the showerhead. He had her body cradled against his chest, trying to keep her as calm as he could.

"Kate, it's Jonathan," he said. "Can you hear me?"

At first he thought he imagined it, but then, slowly, Kate's eyelids rose.

"Kate?" Jake asked, bending slightly to try to level his gaze and grab her attention. It worked.

"I untied her," she whispered. Jonathan's eyebrow rose on reflex. He didn't understand, but apparently Jake did. The agent's entire face fell, but then he gave the smallest of smiles. She tilted her head up to look at Jonathan next.

"I'm glad this isn't a coffin," she said, voice tired.

Jonathan couldn't help but laugh at that.

"Me, too," he said. "How are you feeling?"

Kate quieted a moment, making Jonathan fear that she'd lost consciousness again.

"I feel like I'm the only naked one in here," she finally said, voice notably stronger. Jake laughed this time and retreated into the hotel room. Seconds later he was back with a floor-length robe. Jonathan reached back and turned the water off while the agent held the robe out and closed his eyes.

Kate started to stand, but her legs shook and she couldn't seem to get the hang of it.

"Looks like I need your help still, Mr. Bodyguard," she whispered. Jonathan didn't realize how good it was to hear the sarcastic nickname again. Slowly he stood, bringing Kate with him. Keeping his eyes averted to above her chest so she'd know he wasn't taking advantage of the situation, he helped maneuver her arms into the robe and even tied it once it was closed.

"What time is it?" she asked.

"Almost three," Jonathan answered, still unhappy with how long it had taken to get her the antidote. The two men guided her back to the bed. Jake piled the pillows behind her so she was sitting up straight. He turned to Jonathan after.

"She needs to stay awake for at least a few more hours," he said. "Just in case."

Jonathan nodded.

The agent turned back to his friend.

"How are you feeling, Kate?" he asked, voice kind.

"My body feels tired and my head hurts a little," she admitted. "There's a slight throbbing in my arm, but I suspect that's from the injection."

Jake nodded.

"We were rushed for time. Sorry if I was a little sloppy with it."

Kate shrugged. "I'm not complaining."

She gave the two men a passing smile of gratitude. Jonathan was once again happy to see another sign that Kate was better. The smile didn't last long.

"The EMT," she started, brow creasing. "I think he was the one who injected me."

Jake nodded.

"Jonathan suspected that much. I'm already looking into it."

Kate cast a quick look of surprise at Jonathan before asking the million-dollar question.

"The fact that I'm alive and functioning means that what he pumped into me was my failed drug from years ago, but how did he get it?"

"I'm about to leave to go find that out," Jake said. "But first there are some things I need to tell you that I should have told you sooner."

He turned to Jonathan and he took the hint.

"I'm going to go change while you two talk," he said. "I'll be right next door."

Kate held his gaze with her own dark, mesmerizing eyes before nodding.

Jonathan walked to the adjoining door as Jake began the story about Greg and the FBI's involvement with her research. He wondered how she would take the news.

Jonathan shucked his wet clothes back in his bathroom. He toweled off and took a long, long breath. He'd been a bodyguard for years. He'd taken on clients where nothing out of the ordinary had happened and he'd taken on clients where things had gotten interesting. However, two days with Kathryn Spears and he'd never forget what had happened for the rest of his life. The FBI, secret labs and experimental drugs. He was no longer in his comfort zone as a bodyguard.

But hadn't he already decided that he'd see this contract through? Hadn't he already made a deal with himself that he'd stop at nothing to keep Kate safe?

Jonathan looked at his reflection and nodded to it.

Yes, he had.

He went back to his room and changed into a pair of green khakis and a shirt that was white with a gray trim and went down to his elbows. He ruffled his wet hair and even touched up his goatee with a razor. By the time he stepped into his backup pair of boots, a knock sounded against the adjoining door.

It was Jake. He stepped aside.

"I told her everything," he greeted. "And now that she knows all of the same players as we do, maybe it might help the two of you keep safe. Whoever is behind this, I'm sure they're trying to take what she has before the convention, so I can't stress enough how important it is that that doesn't happen."

"Then why don't we go into some kind of protective custody or, since she's already going to be offered the job, skip the convention altogether?" Jonathan asked.

"Normally that's exactly what I'd do, but we still have no idea who is behind this. Someone had access to the lab and I'm not confident that they wouldn't find out about her protection detail, too. The best I can do is this." Jake went over to the desk and used the complimentary pen and pad to write down an address and number. "On the way over here earlier, after you first called me, I called in a favor to one of the few people I know I can trust. If someone within the Bureau tries to track Kate's or Greg's cell phone, I'll be the first to know. That being said, I can't promise this hotel is safe anymore. I've already told Kate and she turned me down, but this is my apartment. Kate knows where the spare key is." Jonathan took the paper.

"Will she be okay now?"

"I think so." Jake turned for the hotel door, but paused before he opened it. "And Jonathan, what Kate said when she first spoke in the tub…you should ask her what she meant." Jonathan raised his eyebrow at that. "One of the drug's side effects that she experienced when she took it once before was a form of lucid dreaming. I feel like it might do her some good to talk about it." Jake's lips turned up into a small smile. "And you obviously seem to care about her enough to risk some serious jail time. Why else would you, as you said, break into a secret lab for her?"

THE TWO MEN in the other room were undoubtedly smart. Kate knew that much with certainty. However, as she turned her head to try to hear their conversation through the adjoining door, she questioned their intelligence just a bit. Did they really think she couldn't hear them?

"Will she be okay now?" Jonathan asked, sounding as if he was *trying* to be quiet.

Jake responded with an indecisive, "I think so." But Kate knew that if he thought the injection hadn't counteracted the drug, he wouldn't be leaving. Even though he had some quick explaining to do about the man they'd left unconscious in Greg's lab.

Greg's lab.

Kate closed her eyes. Among everything she'd just learned, that was a revelation she hadn't even suspected existed.

"And you obviously seem to care about her enough to risk some serious jail time. Why else would you, as you said, break into a secret lab for her?"

Kate's eyes flashed open. A fluttering actually

moved across her stomach at Jake's words. It was such a foreign feeling of excitement that she tilted her chin down to look at her stomach, as if she could spot a physical object that explained the feeling. But even someone as emotionally stunted as Kate had an inkling of the emotion that made her cheeks heat.

She took a deep breath and slowly let it stream out. The door to Jonathan's room opened and shut. She heard the bodyguard throw the top latch and the dead bolt. For one wild moment Kate became self-conscious of how she looked. With hands that still shook slightly, she felt her hair and sighed again. Without looking at her reflection, she knew the frizz was out of control. It was a nice distraction from the fact that Jonathan had seen and had to touch her naked body. Fleetingly she cursed her past self for canceling her gym membership the year before.

"Can I come in?"

Kate tore herself out of her scattering thoughts and nodded at the man in the doorway. He took the desk chair and rolled it to the side of the bed.

"To be honest, I assumed you wouldn't give me the option of being alone," she admitted. "Considering everything that's happened."

"To be honest, I don't think you want to be alone anymore," he responded. The simple statement made the earlier heat in her cheeks reignite. She held his gaze despite the powerful urge to avert her eyes.

"I'm not afraid to be alone. In fact, I enjoy being alone," she said after a moment. The bodyguard sat up straighter, as if he was ready to highlight all the bad that had happened to point out that she *was* in fact in life-threatening danger and his protection was needed. Kate didn't want to argue. That wasn't the point she was trying to make.

She reached out and took the bodyguard's hand in hers. His skin was warm against her. "But I'm finding that being with you is the exception."

Chapter Sixteen

Jonathan's training throughout the years had helped his reaction time considerably when it came to surprises. Case in point, he'd been able to get Kate out of the way when the car had barreled across the intersection. But as he looked into her eyes while she admitted she wanted to be with him instead of alone, he had no idea how to proceed.

Was she just talking about wanting him around because of his duty as her bodyguard, or was there another truth to her words?

Jonathan felt the walls he'd built around himself try to slide up—to cut off any emotional response to her words—but he didn't have time to think on it for too long. She retracted her hand. Jonathan cleared his throat. The moment, whatever it meant, had passed.

"That was smart of you, by the way," she continued. "Jake said it was your idea to put me under the water to help wake me up faster. Putting me in the shower probably saved my life, or at least its quality."

"Once Jake gave you the injection, you wouldn't

budge. He said it had been too long and if you didn't wake up ASAP you could have some permanent brain damage." Jonathan shrugged. "If I'd had a bucket of water I would have thrown it on you. The shower seemed like a better option. More polite."

Kate laughed a little. It was a good sound to hear.

"Well, thank you," she said. "As far as I can tell, everything up here is as normal as it ever was." She tapped her temple and winced. Jonathan moved closer.

"Are you sure you're okay?" he asked, concern leaking out into every word. Kate rubbed the side of her head but nodded.

"It's just a headache, one I definitely have had before."

"When you took the drug a few years ago," Jonathan supplied. Kate paused the rubbing motion against her head before dropping her hand to her lap.

"Yes. It's like the beginnings of a migraine mixed with the middle of a hangover."

Jonathan made a face.

"That doesn't sound pleasant."

Kate sighed.

"It isn't."

Jonathan contemplated grabbing Kate's hand to ask the next question. He decided against the action but not the question.

"Kate, I know you probably don't want to but—"

"You want to know about the drug," she interjected. He nodded. "You saved my life at least twice today. I suppose the truth is the least you deserve." Jonathan leaned in a fraction. He had a feeling he was about to learn a lot about Kathryn Spears.

"When I was a little girl, I wanted to be a dancer," she started. "A tap dancer, to be precise. I just couldn't get over my love for how the shoes sounded when they hit the ground—I still can't seem to find anything but joy in the sound now." A smile swam up to her lips for a moment. Then it dived back under in the next. "Jake will tell you he always wanted to be in law enforcement—he used to walk around with a plastic badge and pull it out on kids in the playground citing offenses he'd seen them commit—but I think, given time, he would have pursued something like architecture. He had a fixed fascination with building." Kate quieted. While she had offered to finally tell him the truth, she seemed to need some help moving along.

"What changed?" he asked.

"The reason I grew up around Jake was because his father was my mother's partner."

"FBI?" Jonathan guessed. Kate nodded.

"Our parents became good friends and so did we. There were some rough patches at first between my mother and Bill, Jake's father, but they worked it out and had several years of friendship and success. That is, until one night when neither came home." She took a deep breath to seemingly give her strength, but then it seeped out slowly. Jonathan felt a pull in his chest, knowing she was opening a deep wound. "One night turned into two. My mother's car was found abandoned with signs of a struggle and Bill's office had been trashed. I didn't know this at the time. What I also wouldn't learn until later was, while searching my mother's car, they found evidence that she and Bill had been investigating something on the sly. Something that hadn't been reported or sanctioned." She paused and gave a quick smile. "You think I'm stubborn when I'm focused—you should have met my mother." Jonathan couldn't help but return the show of affection. "For the last two years, a lot of their cases fell through last minute. Evidence disappeared. Witnesses suddenly didn't know anything. You name it and it started to happen. Bill and my mother had a theory that someone within their team was behind the scenes, working against them."

"A traitor," Jonathan said.

"Yes. Their boss found their notes and was able to guess the identity of the man. They picked him up and immediately started interrogating him. From what I've been told by my father and Greg, the man let it slip that Mom and Bill were running out of time. They leaned on him until they got an address just outside town. My father had made friends with Mom's boss and was kept in the loop. I remember he called Jake and his mother over to wait. She didn't trust the information, said it was too easy to get." Kate's frown deepened. "She was right. He'd lied, and it wasn't until hours later that he came clean about the real location. My mother's boss called the house to tell them they had a lead. Jake and I overheard the address. It wasn't too far from the house and we knew a shortcut, so we snuck out and rode our bikes there in hopes of saving our parents."

Kate's eyes began to gloss over. She paused to swallow, trying not to cry. Jonathan didn't say a word. He waited as she composed herself.

"To this day, I've never felt the amount of unease I did walking into that warehouse. That feeling where you know something is terribly wrong but can't place it. Jake wanted to leave—he felt it, too—but I was too stubborn. My mother had a saying that just because you were scared didn't mean you weren't strong. And all I was trying to do was be strong." One lone tear slipped out and trailed down her cheek. Before it could keep going, Kate caught it with the back of her other hand. "We found them in the back room. Mom was tied to a chair, beaten badly. Bill was there, too, but in the corner. He wasn't tied up but had been shot—we were told later he'd most likely been trying to save his partner." It was Kate's turn to clear her throat. "We knew the moment we saw them that they were gone, but the kids in us didn't want to believe it. Jake tried to wake up his dad and I tried to untie Mom, as if that would somehow help, but the knots were too tight. I wasn't strong enough."

"'I untied her,'" Jonathan said, quoting her. "That's the first thing you said when you woke up."

Kate nodded.

"I dreamed that I finally freed her. I guess it's been bothering me for a long time." She shrugged. "In the moment I thought if I could untie her, I could have saved her. There was no time, though. Probably less than a minute after we found them, the cavalry showed up. They had enough evidence to send that horrible man away for both of our lives combined, ending his years of betrayal. After all of that, our families stayed together. Jake and I eventually stopped having nightmares, but we knew we had been changed. Jake decided his only goal in life was to become an FBI agent like his father, trading in a plastic badge for the real thing, while I became obsessed with one notion."

Jonathan raised his eyebrow.

"If that man had told the truth the first time he was questioned, Mom and Bill would still be alive."

"That's why you started working on the drug," Jonathan said as he realized.

"I just couldn't get over the fact that one lie destroyed two lives—two families. However, I wasn't so blind with despair to realize that no matter who you are interrogating, there should be an ethical and moral line you don't cross. I know that some would disagree, but, for me, it was important to come up with a non-harmful solution." For the first time Kate gave him a smile that convinced him she was now out of the past. At least the bad parts. "I had a series of lucid dreams in college one month. Ones in which I was a child again and talking to my mother. I told her everything, all of my secrets, without a second thought. I suppose that was because I knew I was dreaming. But that gave me an idea, one that I presented to Greg, who I now realize took it to the FBI. If I could create a drug that replicated the feeling of lucid dreaming, then any question you asked the subject while under its effect would be answered without hesitation."

"Because you trust you're only dreaming," Jonathan guessed.

"Yes. A temporary window in which the person being questioned isn't harmed physically in any way, yet has no imaginable reason why they wouldn't answer the questions asked of them."

"A humane way to interrogate."

Kate nodded. Despite the pride she seemed to take in the idea, her brows drew in together and her lips pursed. Before he could stop the thought, Jonathan imagined the feel of them against his own lips. He shook his head slightly and played it off by cracking his neck.

"The day Greg gave me a physical serum to help remind me of all I'd done was already a bad day. It was the anniversary of Mom and Bill's deaths and frustration took over. As you might have been able to tell, I tend to like my control. Taking the drug, even though I knew it wasn't ready, was my way of trying to get control. Instead, it nearly put me in a coma. It put me in a constant state of lucid dreaming with little hope of ever waking up. Reliving my mother's death over and over again until I died. Not something I want to subject anyone else to. The drug has many years of testing to go before it's ever ready to be used. What Greg gave me in the coffee shop, in the silver case, is another physical copy of the up-to-date drug. A physical representation of everything I've been working toward."

Jonathan sat back in his chair and let out a breath. His last case was sure turning out to be a doozy.

"Sounds like a drug worth trying to steal," he said. From threatening notes before she'd ever left home to nearly being killed by the very drug she'd created, someone wanted what Kate had spent the last five years researching. The couple in the jackets were directly intertwined with that attempt, but Jonathan had a hard time thinking they were doing it alone. When Jonathan and Jake had first gotten into his SUV on the way to the lab, Jonathan had forwarded the picture of the man who had left a note on Kate's door to his phone. Maybe Jake would get lucky and find out his identity. Because the cops still hadn't called him back with any new information.

Just more questions than answers.

KATE'S HEADACHE EXPANDED and consumed. Jonathan's concern seemed to double. It took her several attempts to convince him that the headache was a side effect of both the drug and the fall against the asphalt on the crosswalk. What she needed was some caffeine to help make her feel more alert and normal, something neither of them had.

"I'm not leaving this room," Jonathan said, stern.

"And neither am I," she said, motioning to her robe. "But I'm also hungry."

Kate's stomach growled loudly, egging his decision on. Finally, the bodyguard sighed.

"How about I do this instead?"

He disappeared into his room for a moment. Then she heard him on the phone. She nuzzled back into her pillow, trying to ignore the dull throb that only seemed to be getting worse. She might be able to lose it if she gave in to the urge to sleep, but she'd had enough of that in the last few hours. She loved her mother, but she didn't want to chance reliving her death again any time soon.

Even if Jonathan had been in her dream.

Kate couldn't deny she was more than surprised the bodyguard had made not just one appearance but many within her sleeping mind. From the star lights she'd never owned to the man holding her child form's hand, warning her against all of the badness, saving her from drowning in a self-made coffin, her bodyguard had done his job in both the real world and the one within her mind. She smiled to herself, wondering how she would phrase that in a job performance review.

"Okay, Jett is back on front-desk duty and is personally bringing up the pizza as soon as it gets here. And some coffee for us," Jonathan said. "I'm pretty much not leaving your side until we're on a plane back home. Which should be tomorrow, if you ask me."

Kate put her finger up and placed it against his mouth. It was an impulsive, harmless move on her part, but the feel of his lips against her skin sent a shock through her. One that wasn't unpleasant in the least. Jonathan's body tensed. Had he felt it, too?

"Jonathan," she started, voice much softer than she'd meant it to be. "Let's not talk about this until we've at least eaten. Please."

Jonathan's eyes searched her face. The self-consciousness she'd felt earlier wasn't there anymore. The way he was looking at her somehow made her feel oddly beautiful. She lowered her finger, dropping her hand back to her lap. The corner of his lips pulled up.

"Okay, Miss Scientist," he said. "Now, I'm going to go check in with the boss to let her know we're okay. While we were at the lab, she sent quite a few texts. And, before you ask, no, I'm not going to tell her everything that's going on. Not until we figure out who's behind this. I don't want to put her or Orion in any unnecessary danger."

Kate watched him go back into his room. The adjoining door she'd loathed the day before had become an unforeseen perk.

Giving him privacy, as much as she could while being so close, Kate tried to clear her mind and relax. Or something similar given that relaxing wasn't possible under the circumstances. She focused on her breathing and it seemed to work. She didn't even realize when Jonathan started talking or when the knock sounded against his door.

However, she didn't miss the sound of someone's body slamming into the wall.

Kate moved out of bed as quickly as she could. The

sound of another body hitting the wall made her pause, frozen in the middle of the room.

"Jonathan?" she asked into the quiet that followed. There was a shuffling noise and the bodyguard appeared in the doorway.

"You're bleeding," Kate said, looking to the blood on his lip. He shook off the concern.

"Get into the bathroom and lock the door. He's here."

Chapter Seventeen

Kate wanted to complain—wanted to help—but she realized her running into whatever fray there was in the next room wouldn't help anything. She did as she was told and retreated to the bathroom, locking the door behind her. The floor was still wet and cold against her bare feet, but her attention was outside the room. *He* as in the man who had left the note?

What was he doing here now?

No sooner had she questioned it than her stomach dropped. The woman who had driven the car over Greg had been aiming at her. If she showed up with the man again, then it was safe to assume he wasn't there to sit down and chat.

Kate strained as she tried to listen to what was happening in the next hotel room. No sound was getting through. Worry about Jonathan crept into her mind and exploded. Which only intensified when a door in the next room slammed shut.

Kate held her breath and waited.

A pounding sound began on the other side, but not

against the bathroom door. Whoever had slammed the adjoining door between rooms must have been in her room now. Which meant whoever was still in Jonathan's room must have been trying to get in hers.

The question now was, who was in there with her?

Before she could weigh the pros and cons of flinging open the door and checking on Jonathan, hoping it was him on the other side, someone tried the door handle.

Kate nearly screamed. The lock wasn't sticking. The handle began to move and slowly the door began to open. Whoever was behind it wasn't Jonathan. He would have called out to her, that much Kate was certain. So, with mounting terror, she turned and threw her back against the door, shutting it the small distance it had opened.

A man cursed loudly on the other side.

Definitely not Jonathan.

Kate braced her feet against the slick tile and waited for the man to try again. But how long could she really keep the door closed?

Looking around the room, she tried to spot something that could be used as a weapon. The only thing that looked remotely dangerous was the towel rack. It was too far away and she doubted she'd be able to pull it free from the wall. Feeling increasingly defeated, Kate's eyes traveled across the counter next to her.

And stopped.

Reaching out, she grabbed her travel-size hair spray. Quickly she tossed off the cap. The man slammed into the door hard. Kate tried to push against it, using her legs to apply pressure backward, but he was stronger. In a last-ditch effort at self-defense, Kate put her finger on the nozzle and jumped away from the door, flattening herself against the wall.

The bathroom door flung open. If the rubber doorstop hadn't been attached to the wall, the handle would have made one big hole. The man stopped just inside the room. For one moment they looked at each other.

It was the man who had followed them and who was on the hotel security footage. Without his coat he stood tall and well-built and looked quite a deal younger than she had originally suspected—perhaps early thirties. Like her, he had dark eyes and hair. Unlike her, he was smiling. Kate didn't wait to find out what his plans were.

Wielding the only weapon she had, Kate sprang forward and sprayed the hair spray at the man's face. It was a move he hadn't expected, and even though he grabbed the front of her robe and slung her into the hallway, she'd hit her target. It was a delayed reaction but one that wasn't lacking. The man let out a yell and let her go, fisting at his eyes. Kate used his pain to her advantage. She moved her foot up and connected hard with his groin.

He doubled over, a stream of expletives bursting from his lips. Kate backed up to the wall and moved along it until she was at the door to the hallway. The pounding she'd heard earlier became louder, terrifying her even more and scattering her thoughts, seconds before a loud crack. Kate already had the door open, one foot in the hallway, when another crack followed. She started to turn to place the sound when a ding from the elevators floated down the hallway. If she could get someone to call security, that would strengthen their chances against the unnamed assailant.

However, they weren't so lucky.

The woman, counterpart to the man bellyaching in the room behind her and driver of the car that had put Greg in the hospital, walked off the elevator and fixed Kate with a stare that made her blood run cold. For a moment all Kate could hear was the soft hum of the hallway lights.

She too appeared to be younger than Kate had once thought. Her hair was dark blond and even from the distance between them she saw dark eyes that narrowed at her. In her right hand was a gun.

"Well, hello, Miss Spears."

And then she lifted the gun and shot.

THE DOOR DIDN'T fly off its hinges or break clean in half, but as Jonathan kicked out with all the force he could summon after being temporarily knocked off his feet, the door between his room and Kate's gave way. It splintered unevenly, making him work more to clear the debris until he was standing in his room, fuming.

When he'd gone to answer the door, he'd looked through the peephole to see someone he thought was Jett. The glass was more foggy than clear and Jonathan's mind was still on his call with Nikki. He'd been distracted and it had cost him. Less than a second after he'd opened the door, the man who had delivered the bloody letter had pushed inside. They'd fought in the small hallway and Jonathan had been lucky to land a good hit that dazed the man, giving him enough time to warn Kate. When he'd returned, the man was ready. His fists dealt out blows that Jonathan hadn't been prepared to receive. Especially the right hook that had knocked him dizzy.

By the time Jonathan had regained his footing, the man had slammed the adjoining door shut. The key cards able to open the door were both on Kate's dresser.

Now Jonathan stood in the hotel room with a heaving chest, looking at a scene he didn't quite understand. The man was outside the bathroom, hunched over and cursing. His eyes moved up to Jonathan but they were angry red slits. The bathroom door behind him was open and Kate was nowhere to be seen.

Jonathan wanted to smile, realizing that the scientist had fought back and disabled her attacker, at least temporarily. But what happened next pushed any victorious thoughts clear from his mind.

A gun went off in the hallway.

Kate!

The man, despite struggling with the pain inflicted on him by Kate, whipped his head around to the door so fast that Jonathan thought he heard it snap. Apparently he wasn't the only one caught off guard by the discharge. Jonathan rushed the man.

He might have been hurt, his eyes might have been watering, but the dark-haired man wasn't down for the count. He turned and ducked out of the way at the last second. The hit he couldn't land left Jonathan exposed in front of him, giving the man an easy target. Much like Jonathan did to the door, the intruder hiked his leg up and pushed his foot against Jonathan's stomach. The force sent him back into the wall. A cracking sound split the air as a part of the wall gave out under his weight.

Jonathan let out a groan that hitched a ride on the pain pulsing through his body. But that didn't mean he was down for the count, either. He pushed off the wall with his elbows and threw a punch. The man brought up his arms in time for the hit to be absorbed by his forearms. Still, it did enough to push him back, stepping into the bathroom.

Jonathan came at him again, not wanting to lose the small momentum he had gained. He torqued his left arm back before moving it around to make a solid arc. Imagining, as he always did, going *through* the target and not simply *to* it, he pictured his fist going clean through the man's jaw. It worked. The skin of his knuckles kissed the man's jaw with hot anger, a hit he couldn't dodge. As though the sound of the impact alone was powerful enough, he staggered backward. Jonathan moved closer, ready to keep going, when the man's struggle to remain standing failed. His shoes slipped on the water pooled on the floor, sending his feet flying out from beneath him. He hit the tile hard and his head hit the lip of the tub with a smack. The man's head lolled to the side and the rest of him went

limp. Whether the man was dead or simply unconscious, Jonathan didn't have time to find out. He ran
out of the hotel room and into the empty hallway. Relief that Kate wasn't lying on the ground anywhere in
sight made him exhale. But where was she now?

Their new hotel rooms were between the elevators
and the stairs. He took off to the left, hoping she'd
gone that direction instead of toward the other stairs.

He needed to find her.

He needed to protect her.

He needed her to be safe.

The doors to the elevator slid open as he neared the
end of the hall. An older man with a straw fedora and
a smart blue suit looked wide-eyed at him as he flew
past. Before Jonathan could warn him that it wasn't
safe, another gunshot sounded. The man shrank back
into the elevator and pressed the Close Door button
while Jonathan tore open the door to the stairs.

"Kate?" he yelled. His voice echoed off the concrete.
The stairwell was too small for him to see to the floors
below or the one above. No one replied. He started to
run down the steps, but then stopped and reversed his
path, going to the fourth floor, convinced that that was
where the shot had come from. Why had Kate gone up
instead of down?

Jonathan pushed open the door just as someone else
was trying to open it.

"Kate," he exclaimed, more relief than he thought
possible exploding within him at the sight of her. She

rocked back on her heels, surprised, and clambered for his hands. He gave them, helping to steady her.

"Run," she said, breathless.

Another gunshot—louder, too close for comfort—added emphasis to the command. Jonathan pulled Kate into the stairwell and guided her along with him back down the steps to the third-floor landing. He pushed them through the door while Kate sucked in a breath. Jonathan glanced back at her and barely caught her as she stumbled forward.

"Dizzy," she wheezed out.

He looped his arm around her middle and pulled up to support some of her weight as they continued to move toward their rooms. Jonathan knew there was a chance that the man was still alive and kicking, but he also knew that man hadn't had a gun. Or at least wasn't willing to use it like his partner. Plus, running down narrow hallways wasn't going to do them any good. Not with Kate unable to run on her own.

Jonathan reached for his key card in his back pocket when another kink in his ever-evolving plan popped up. The door to Kate's room began to open. He let out a long stream of expletives as he used all his power to hoist Kate's body up and keep running down the hall. The fast escape he wanted to make turned into less of a run and more of a pained jog.

"Don't shoot, you idiot," the man behind them yelled seconds after the stairwell door banged open. Jonathan didn't dare look back. Not even when he swung Kate around, using his body as a shield, and hit the elevator

Down button. Their one dose of good luck came at the sound of a beep as the doors slid open seconds later.

"Get them," a woman yelled from farther away. It was the confirmation Jonathan needed that the woman who had run over Greg was also after Kate.

Jonathan punched the Lobby button and the Close Door button while flattening Kate against the wall with his body. The doors slowly began to close. He felt Kate exhale, her entire body relaxing against him. Once they got to the lobby he'd be able to hide her until the cops came. He'd be able to keep her safe.

When there was less than a sliver left of open space between the closing doors, a hand snaked through. Jonathan jumped forward, trying to push the man out, but the doors opened enough for him to push inside. Jonathan fully expected him to keep the doors open for his gun-wielding friend, but he surprised him.

The dark-haired man hit the Close Door button. His partner yelled angrily as they slid shut. Jonathan reached out and pulled Kate over to him, moving her once again behind his back. The man across from them let out a devilish smile.

"My friend doesn't like sticking to the plan," he said. "But don't worry, I do."

Chapter Eighteen

Kate screamed.

The man's fist connected with Jonathan's cheek while his other hand reached for Kate. He managed to grab a fistful of her hair, but before he could pull, Jonathan hit above his elbow in an impressive rendition of a karate chop. It generated enough pain that the man let go of her hair, but not before yanking down. She barely had time to yell before Jonathan threw his forearm out to keep her pinned to the wall. He didn't want her anywhere near their attacker.

And she didn't, either.

The man recovered quickly and sent a volley of attacks at the bodyguard. Instead of dodging them, though, Jonathan used the hand not grabbing Kate to cover his face. The man had them in the corner, and if Jonathan so much as moved an inch to either side, he'd hit Kate square on.

Jonathan was protecting her and getting hurt in the process.

She didn't like that.

Not one bit.

The elevator dinged as they slowed to the lobby. The man, in one last desperate attempt, hit Jonathan so hard in the ribs that he doubled over. It left Kate open to him once again. He lunged forward and grabbed her hair. She fumbled in the pocket of her robe for her travel-size hair spray. If she could get his eyes again, then Jonathan could take him out.

"Not again," the man growled when she held the bottle up. He yanked her hair hard toward him, walking backward out of the now-open elevator doors. The pain from her headache intertwined with the burn from her hair being pulled created a wave of nausea. She lost her focus and the hair spray hit the ground.

"Help," she yelled. Murmurs from the lobby turned into shouts. The man moved quickly, dragging her along by her hair. She couldn't see the people around her and she couldn't see the anger on her bodyguard's face.

But she could hear it.

Large footfalls moved around her before the sound of someone being used as a punching bag met her ears. Soon after, her attacker released his hold. Kate fell on her backside, whipping her head up, ready for the next attack. What she saw instead was Jonathan pulling the man's dark hair, both of their faces bloodied.

"Doesn't feel good, does it?" Jonathan bit out. He punched, but was knocked to the side by another well-aimed kick from the man. Kate looked around the lobby to the handful of bystanders. An elderly couple sat on the couch closest to the windows facing the street, two teens stood with a man who had his hands full of luggage and a young mother guarding her toddler at the front desk began moving away. Kate expected someone to step forward but no one did. Until a man yelled from the front door.

"The cops are on their way," Jett warned. Just on the tail of his announcement was the sweet, sweet chorus of sirens in the distance. The man grappling with Jonathan didn't miss the new information. His attacks became faster, trying to break Jonathan down in the limited amount of time he had left.

Thankfully, Jett wasn't done helping yet. He ran up to the fray and tried to pull the man off the bodyguard. His fearless act inspired a chain reaction. The father of the teens dropped his bags and jumped in, too. They disengaged the unknown man from Jonathan just as the elderly man from the window stood up.

"I can see them comin'," he called.

The realization that the cops were nearly there and it was now three against one seemed to finally push a flight instead of fight response in the attacker. Jett tried to grab for him again but he moved quickly, and he moved around the father as he tried, too. Apparently the man was strong *and* fast.

Kate could see Jonathan getting ready to run after the man who was heading toward the front door. His body had already tilted forward a fraction, more than ready to do whatever he could to stop their attacker.

But Kate couldn't claim the same thing.

She didn't want her bodyguard to get hurt anymore. Not because of her.

"Jonathan," she called out. He turned and she nearly stopped breathing. His eyes were filled with an anger so intense some of the feeling transferred to her. She took in his injuries—his busted bottom lip, bruised jaw, split eyebrow—and felt a fury she didn't think could ever be extinguished. Whoever was behind all of this, whoever the couple was, they would get their due. That train of thought was nearly doused by the cold that crept in. "Jonathan, what about the woman?"

Jonathan's eyes widened. Kate knew he wouldn't leave her now, not even to chase down the man. He quickly yelled to Jett about the woman with the gun. Then Jett ushered the people in the lobby behind the front desk and into the part of the building only accessible to employees. Jonathan picked Kate up off the floor and helped her along with them.

"Are you okay?" Jonathan asked as soon as they stopped moving. He held her chin up so her gaze had no other place to go. And maybe she didn't want to look anywhere else, either.

"I am now," she said honestly. It created a reaction in his face she couldn't quite place. She felt her brows pull together in question. "What about you?" She started to reach out—to hold *his* face and make sure *he* was okay—when Jett hurried over to them.

"We called the cops when we heard the first shot," he said. "We also can't find Arthur."

"Arthur?" Kate and Jonathan asked in unison.

"The security guard on shift. He wasn't back here, so—"

A door down the hallway opened with such force the sound echoed throughout the lobby. On what had to be reflex Jonathan moved Kate around him again. The teens' father did the same with his kids and the elderly couple, putting them behind him. Jett even stepped back to put himself in front of the young mother and her toddler. Everyone seemed to be holding his or her breath until a woman walked around the corner.

It was the hotel manager, Lola Teague, and she was clearly fired up.

"I just watched that woman on the security camera go out the fire exit in the kitchen," she said. Her hair, which had been impeccable the night before, was now visibly ruffled. The laugh lines at the edge of each eye definitely were not being exercised. "I'd ask for everyone's calm and patience as we deal with this matter quickly." The sound of the sirens could be heard clearly from where they stood. Soon the cops would be in the lobby. Lola hurried to the door, pausing just long enough to whisper to them. "Whoever that couple is, they sure are determined."

Lola had no idea.

THE COPS WHO had come the day before for the letter were much more interested in what Jonathan and Kate had to say this time around. While they decided not to reveal that Kate had been drugged earlier in the day, they didn't stop from pointing out what had also happened at the crosswalk. Even a rookie cop could see there was a connection there.

"We ran the picture of that man through our criminal database but didn't get anything," one of them admitted. "The blood was real, but we got no match. But now that we have his accomplice on camera, we should be able to get a name."

Should and *would* were two very different things, but Kate kept her mouth shut. The officers didn't know the entire story, so how did she expect them to do their jobs?

Frustrated, Kate cracked the seal of the bottle of water she'd been handed. Her decision to pursue a drug that could potentially save lives in situations where time was the enemy was one she'd never regretted. Even now she couldn't come to second-guess it. When something consumes your life that much, for so long, the mind begins to treat it like a piece of the foundation that makes you who you are. Part of who Kate was, intrinsically tied to her life, was a drug that turned life into a dream.

"Oh, my God," Kate breathed out, nearly choking on her water. Jonathan stood a foot or so away, still in the lobby, talking with Lola. When he heard her, he did a U-turn so fast it almost made her dizzy again.

"What's wrong?"

She stood, stronger than before, but nowhere near as agile as she wanted.

"The case," was all she said.

It was enough.

Jonathan took her by her elbow and maneuvered her into the elevator. The one they hadn't fought in. She replayed what had happened in the other before recalling all other attacks that had taken place that day.

"I don't understand," Kate started. Jonathan didn't turn his gaze to her. He was more than focused on the elevator doors. Or, more aptly, what might jump out at them when they opened. "The woman would have killed me with her car had you not pushed me out of the way. She'd also have shot me had I not been able to stumble to the stairs. The man, though, seemed to want to take me with him." The elevator reached the third floor. Jonathan angled his body in front of her again. He stepped out, a man born of cautiousness, and nodded when it was clear. He resumed his position at her elbow. "So they don't seem to be on the same page. Plus, killing me wouldn't benefit anyone. I'm no longer, and really never was, the sole researcher of the drug. However..."

They stopped outside her hotel room. Jonathan pulled out the key card.

"I might be the only one with the prototype."

Jonathan did his due diligence again, heading in first and clearing the room before Kate stepped inside. She took in the details of a few holes in the wall where the men must have struggled and the water pooled on the bathroom tile.

"I thought he was dead," Jonathan reiterated, pointing to the tub. "I thought he broke his neck, but I was wrong."

Kate patted the bodyguard on the shoulder and went straight for the bed. She started to bend down but became dizzy. Jonathan was at her side in a flash.

"I'm okay," she said, shooing away his hands. "Is the case there?"

Before he bent down to look, she already knew it wasn't. Why go through all of that trouble without a parting gift?

Jonathan shook his head.

"What could they do with it, really?" he asked.

Kate shrugged. "Destroying it would be useless, since it can be replicated with the research. Using it, or selling it, would be a one-shot deal, and honestly, we don't even know if it works. There's a high chance that it'll have the same effect that the earlier stage of the drug had. My guess would be whoever they are, they're trying to reverse engineer it. Break it down to figure out what's inside so they can make more. Then again, if they have access to the labs, they wouldn't need to go through all that trouble."

"Well, what if we are wrong about that?" Kate raised her eyebrow. "What if they don't have access to the lab? What if it isn't an inside job? What if we know too much and it's skewing our perception of everything that's happened?"

Kate's mouth dangled open a fraction, making her guess she looked like a cartoon character. She could tell her surprise confused him. He tilted his head, giving her a questioning look.

"What?" he asked.

"That was just really attractive," she admitted before she could censor herself. Jonathan broke into a grin that only made him more mouthwatering.

"What? Objective thinking or problem solving?"

Kate felt her cheeks burn, but she laughed.

"Both."

Jonathan joined in. When the laughter died a moment later, he took a step toward her. Something in the chemistry of the moment changed. The heat from her cheeks burned hotter. She hadn't been with a man in so long and not just in an intimate way. Jonathan Carmichael was looking at her like she'd seen other men look at other women, seeing not just a physical body but also a potential future. What could he see when looking at her?

Kate averted her gaze. This wasn't the time to find out.

"We need to call Jake and tell him what happened," she said. "If you're right and these people didn't have access to the lab, then finding out how they got the failed drug may be the key to figuring out what's going on. Plus, now that we have the woman's picture, maybe he can use the FBI database to find out who she is."

Kate didn't look up to see if Jonathan agreed. Instead she turned to the dresser. Opening the top drawer, she moved past her intimate apparel and pulled out a screwdriver.

"Should I be worried about why you had that in there?" Jonathan asked. Kate turned with a half smile. Whatever their moment had been, it had reverted back to normal. She moved over to the air-conditioning unit and got on her knees. She began to unscrew its cover.

"My mother taught me many things at a young age. Like how it's important to protect the things you care about. And how, sometimes, that means we must hide those very things." She removed the last screw and gently took off the cover. Taped to the inside was a small Moleskine notebook. Gingerly she removed it. Jonathan came to stand beside her, looking down at the book. "While I had digital files on what I was working on, I didn't put them all in the computer. I was always afraid that somehow the information might be leaked." She shook the notebook. "So I kept a secret hard copy that detailed everything. If our mystery crew has no access to the lab and its notes, then *this* is what they should have taken."

"And if they find out you have that, they might pay us another visit," Jonathan breathed out. He sounded split between anger and exhaustion.

Kate flipped open the notebook and let her eyes trace her handwritten scrawls. Notes, figures and calculations she'd devoted the past five years to—but really, her whole life.

A part of her.

A part of her mother.

And now a part of Jonathan.

Chapter Nineteen

Jake didn't answer his phone when Kate called and they decided against leaving any specific information on his voice mail. A vague "Call as soon as you get this—we need to talk," was all the scientist said. Still, Jonathan parked his rental outside an apartment complex on the Upper East Side of Manhattan with every intention of making it their permanent residence until they left New York.

"His apartment is on the third floor," Kate said, pulling her luggage over the sidewalk and up to the front door. No longer in her robe, she'd changed into a long-sleeved blue blouse, a pair of jeans and comfortable-looking flats. She twisted her hair up into a bun and had taken pains to spray down her thick bangs. She hadn't fooled with applying makeup. It was nearing night and they'd be staying put.

"You've been here before, right?" Jonathan asked as he helped her inside. Immediately they were met with stairs to their right. Kate exhaled.

"Yes, once, which means I sadly know there's no elevator. Because I haven't already had my fill of stairs for today," she mumbled. "At least now I won't be getting shot at."

Jonathan smiled, thinking her frustration was perhaps a great deal cuter than it should have been, and started the trek upward, all the while fussing over the woman like she was a child. She'd already been the target of attempted murder three times in two days. Jonathan reasoned his worry was more than warranted.

There were four apartments on the third floor and Kate directed them to one facing the street they'd parked on. A brown and black doormat with the word *Welcome* greeted them.

"Surely an FBI agent doesn't just keep his spare key beneath the mat?" he asked, worrying that maybe Jake wasn't as careful as he'd thought.

Kate chuckled. She lowered her bags to the ground. Putting her foot on the black rubber part of the mat, she bent and burrowed her fingers beneath the raised brown plastic on top. She pulled up and the sound of Velcro coming apart followed.

"It's not Fort Knox, but I don't think many would look here," she said, spying the key tucked in the open space. She pushed the middle back down and turned to Jonathan. Her eyebrow arched.

"Are you jealous of Jake's doormat?"

Jonathan rolled his eyes.

"Just unlock the door."

The apartment opened on a small L-shaped white kitchen that attached directly to the living area with an exposed brick accent wall at the back. Between the two was a small square dining set, a dark green patterned couch, a barrel that had been converted into an accent table and a large flat screen atop shelving bolted into the brick. On the rest of the walls making up the living and dining space were various framed pictures ranging from posters of cop movies to random road signs to pictures of family and friends. Kate watched as Jonathan took in these details and elaborated on a few.

"The only rebellious phase Jake ever went through when we were younger was stealing street signs. He's quite proud of them still." Her attention moved to the converted table. "That was a gag gift my father got Bill a year before he died. I don't think Jake's ever been without it." She pointed to the door across from the table. It was small, as he guessed the room behind it also would be. "Guest bedroom," she said, then pointed to the door next to it. "Very tiny, badly tiled bathroom. Leaving the last door as his room. Also not the most attractive room."

Jonathan laughed and parked his bags next to the couch. He headed back to the kitchen. Their pizza had never shown up at the hotel and he hoped Jake had something that could pass as a meal.

Kate dropped her things off in the guest bedroom and disappeared into Jake's room soon after. To do what, he didn't know. The agent didn't have anything to make a three-course meal, but he had enough to make turkey sandwiches with a side of chips. Jonathan didn't know much about Kate's eating habits aside from her love of the Chinese restaurant, but he was almost positive she was as hungry as he was and would take the food without complaint.

"Food's ready," he called, plating each sandwich.

Kate appeared as he put the plates on the dining table. Her cheeks were rosy and she didn't meet his eyes right away.

"You look suspicious," he commented. Kate tried to play coy and waved a hand at him as if to bat away his concern. "What did you do?"

"Nothing," she said, as if pretending she hadn't gone into the agent's room in the first place. She took her seat across from him. He was happy to see the flash of pleasure that crossed her face as she spied the food. She didn't hesitate in beginning to eat.

"You know, I don't think I've snooped through Mark's or Oliver's places before, which is what I'm assuming you just did, and definitely not Nikki's," he pointed out with a smile. "I think you're nosy."

"From the little I know of Nikki Waters, it's probably a good thing you don't," she replied, not denying the accusation. "I would think the founder of a security agency appreciates her privacy." He gave her a thumbs-up to show she was right on the money. "I only snoop when I think there might be something worthy of the effort." She cut her eyes back to Jake's room. "Something that might help us make sense of everything."

"And did you find anything useful?"

"No, but I didn't really have enough time, now did I?" She threw him a wink that induced a different kind of pleasure within him than when Kate had eyed her food. It caught him off guard. So much so that he tried to cover for whatever his expression might have given away. He turned to the pictures on the wall beside them.

"Is that Bill?" he asked, honing in on one of a dark blond-haired man smiling wide. The ocean was behind him and he squinted a bit from the glare of the sun. The picture was aged.

"Yes, that was a few years before—" Kate stopped that thought and continued with a new one. "I think my father was the one who took that picture, actually." She put her half-eaten sandwich down and stood. She went along the wall, nose close, investigating each picture until she found the one she was looking for. "Our parents decided to do a joint family vacation one year. It had been a long time since Jake's mom had been to the beach, so we packed up for a few days and went."

Jonathan joined her in front of the picture. Bill was sitting in the sand behind Jake as a little boy, while a smiling fair-haired woman was farther back in a striped beach chair. Jake wasn't looking at the camera, his concentration on a half-constructed sand castle in front of him. Jonathan recognized Deacon from Kate's Orion file—the younger version was seated in his own striped chair next to Jake's mother, caught in midlaugh. A woman in a black one-piece stood near him, but her eyes were on the little girl with her hands in the sand castle, a small smile on her face. That little girl, undoubtedly Kate, was the only person in the picture looking directly at the camera. They all looked so happy. So content. "You look just like your mother," Jonathan said, looking back at the woman. When the picture was taken she'd been older than Kate was now, but the resemblance was unbelievable.

Kate smiled.

"Thank you. This was actually the first attempt at a nice, smiling picture another tourist was kind enough to offer to take, but then something made my father break out into laughter." The smile from receiving Jonathan's compliment extended. It seemed to strengthen with the power of what must have been a good memory. "After that no one could get their acts together. I don't even know that we have a normal one. A few years back Jake's mother found this and made copies for us and my dad. It's one of my favorite pictures." Kate turned and Jonathan felt the bright light of the love she felt for her family, including Jake and his parents, move to him. Inadvertently he took a step away. He wished he could share the same type of memories—childhood ones of family—with her, be able to share stories of growing up, even the bumps along the way. But he had none.

He moved back to the table and picked up his food again. He was aware that Kate watched him, but she didn't comment on the change in his mood. Instead she, too, went back to eating, and in silence they each finished their food. Still without talking, Kate collected their empty plates and cleaned up. Jonathan tried to shake the mood he'd fallen into but was coming up short. The walls—the emotional barriers—around him built up once again. So high, in fact, that he didn't notice when Kate took her seat opposite him again until she spoke.

"Foster care?" Jonathan felt his eyes widen, finding hers with a questioning look. She gave him an apologetic smile and explained, "Yesterday you mentioned you moved around a lot as a child, something that you seemed angry about but not annoyed with. You also have an intense desire to plant roots and a fierce loyalty and, I bet, protectiveness of your friends and Orion. You talk about them as if they are your family. Plus—" she motioned to the back of her upper arm "—your tattoo. It's of a house."

"That's a big assumption you're making," he said. His even tone didn't faze her. Her dark eyes were kind, searching his face for what, he didn't know. She remained quiet until finally he decided to tell her a story he'd never told anyone before. "My mom died right after I was born and my dad had no business being a parent. So he decided not to be." The anger that he had once felt—the resentment—toward his father all of his childhood wasn't there anymore. He was just stating facts now.

"Like thousands of other children in the country, I was never adopted and constantly moved around through foster families. For one reason or another, I couldn't make a meaningful connection with the adults. I couldn't seem to make friends with any of the kids, either. Not that it would matter if I had. There were some kids who had siblings in the system they hadn't seen or talked to in years." He exhaled. He might no longer feel the ill feelings he once had about his father's abandonment, but he didn't think he'd ever forget the overwhelming weight of loneliness.

"In high school I was sent to live with a woman who was rumored to only get kids with no hope of being adopted," he continued. "I'll never forget her, if only for her tattoos. She had these large, intricate works of art covering almost every inch of skin. One day I asked how she picked them. She said it had started with one. She'd sat down and thought about what she loved or wanted most in life and got a tattoo that represented it. Every one after was something else she loved or wanted until she was running out of room. So, one day I sat down, too, and while I was trying to think of what I loved more than anything, I drew this." He turned a bit so she could see the tattoo better. He didn't have to look down to recall the little box outline with its triangle on top, squares for windows and a small rectangle for the front door. It was an exact replica of the one he'd doodled on the corner of his notebook. "I guess I'm a cliché. The only thing I'd ever loved was the idea of a home."

Kate stood up so quickly that her chair scraped against the hardwood. Jonathan tensed, ready to put out whatever fire she'd just remembered, but the brunette came around the table and threw her arms around him. She put her chin against his shoulder and buried her face against his neck.

"You're not a cliché," she said, slightly muffled.

Jonathan felt the walls around him shake. Not on reflex—because he didn't have one for this kind of situation—he returned the embrace with a smile. Kate's body was warm against him. The perfume she'd put on before they'd left the hotel was flowery and perfect.

"Thank you," he said, voice soft, almost afraid to spook her. Kate stepped back and what Jonathan saw alarmed him. "Are you crying?"

Kate brought the back of her hands up and wiped away the few stray tears that had found their way to her reddened cheeks.

"Well, excuse me," she exclaimed. "My heartstrings were just violently strummed." She started to move away from him, backing up like she'd been burned. He'd embarrassed her.

"No," he said, capturing her hands so she couldn't escape. "I just don't want to see you cry. Not because of me." Kate stopped moving. Another tear leaked out and all Jonathan could think about was stopping it. He dropped her hand and lifted it to her cheek, running his fingers across and wiping the tear free. "I'll admit that my childhood wasn't ideal, and there are times when I still wish it had been different, but then I remember if it had, I never would have met Nikki. She never would have referred me for a job at Redstone and I'd never have met Oliver and Mark. I'd never leave and join Orion and meet some of the best people I've ever known."

He heard his voice go low on the last part, saw

Kate's expression soften and felt the urge to tell her she was now included in that list of people all at the same time. "Don't worry about me, Kate. Let me worry about you."

Chapter Twenty

Every part of Kate was telling—no, screaming at—her to kiss the man in front of her. To create a different kind of embrace than the one they'd shared moments before. To open up and lose herself in something other than her work.

But Kate's body drew away from him before her mind could reason out why. She gave him a quick smile she hoped said everything she couldn't and moved out of his reach.

"The convention is tomorrow afternoon, and no matter what happens, I feel like I should get some sleep," she said.

It was like a fog lifted from Jonathan's face. He straightened his back, cleared his throat and nodded. Guilt, though she didn't quite understand its place, slowly turned within her. Like she'd deflated him somehow.

"Yeah, I don't blame you for being tired," he said. "I'm going to stay out here and wait for Jake to get in."

"Could you wake me up when he does?" Kate was

already moving away, as if she could physically separate herself from the foreign feeling of desire she realized had started to grow.

"Sure thing," he said, "Good night, Miss Scientist."

Despite her unease, when she got to the guest bedroom door she turned with a quick response.

"You, too, Mr. Bodyguard."

She shut the door behind her like she was running from a nightmare. But hadn't Jonathan been the one good thing in her dreams? Kate put her back to the door and tried to compose her skittering thoughts.

The man had opened up to her—had been undeniably vulnerable—and what had she done with the moment? Run. The way he'd looked at her, the way he'd wiped her tears away yet left his hand caressing her face had given her the perfect moment to grab hold of something.

But she couldn't do it.

Jonathan wanted roots. He wanted friends, a family, a home. Aside from her father visiting and the occasional email or phone call from Greg and Jake, Kate's life revolved around her work. Her one goal in life. She didn't know how to cope or deal with anything else. Like her father said, she was narrow-minded. Seeing the big picture wasn't just hard for her, it was sometimes downright impossible.

One thing she was sure of in the midst of all of the new uncertainty that had surfaced in her life was that the man in the next room deserved more than an emotionally stunted woman stumbling through what others did with ease.

He deserved a life without her as a complication.

KATE ROLLED OVER, getting wrapped up in the mismatched blanket and sheets, and looked up into the darkness. She'd been in bed for at least two hours and hadn't gotten a lick of sleep, but not for lack of trying.

The first hour she wondered if it was her fear of slipping back into her dream world from earlier that day. Reliving the discovery of her mother and Bill's bodies was frightening enough to make her mind try its best to stay awake. It was a niggling thought that finally got her to call her father. She'd ignored his few calls over the last two days, responding with a quick text that she was fine, just busy. She didn't want to worry him more than he already was. Despite the late hour, which she let him assume was because she'd been working and lost track of time, he'd been happy to finally hear her voice. She promised to call him after the convention the next day. She made sure to tell him she loved him. The rest of that hour had then crawled by. Yet, as she rolled into the next hour, she started to realize what she was really afraid of.

The dark.

The world when she was awake.

The couple that had made very public and violent attempts on her life.

Thoughts of the man and his dark, narrow eyes made her hand flit to her hair. She massaged her scalp, remembering the pain of having her hair pulled without an ounce of remorse.

It was that man and his partner that kept her tossing and turning. The tiny window that faced the side of the building next door didn't help with its lack of light that filtered into the small room.

After more time had passed, Kate finally gave up. As quietly as if it was Christmas and she was trying to get a glimpse of Santa, she tiptoed to the door and slowly opened it. She winced as it creaked something awful. The lights from the kitchen and living area were off, save for a floor lamp next to the TV. It was enough light for her to see Jonathan quickly turn at the noise.

She held her hands up in defense.

"Sorry," she whispered. "I meant to be a bit sneakier than that."

Jonathan visibly relaxed and put down what looked like a sports magazine he'd been reading.

"Is everything okay?"

Kate nodded.

"You having trouble sleeping?"

Jonathan grinned.

"I'm not trying to."

"You have to sleep sometime," she pointed out.

"Sometimes that's not in the job description."

Kate was going to argue, but who was she to tell anyone what to do within the bounds of their job. She certainly didn't listen to others. Still, she bounced from foot to foot, trying carefully to say the right thing.

"So," she started, cheeks already blazing hot. "You're not going to try to sleep any time soon?"

Jonathan raised his eyebrow but nodded.

"I've worked on a lot less sleep," he explained. "Why?"

Kate's blush was an all-out inferno. She could feel its heat even moving to her ears.

"Well, I was wondering, if it's okay with you, if maybe you could come stay in here with me?" Jonathan's eyebrow rose so high that it almost seemed to get lost in his hairline. "It's just, well, I can't fall asleep," she added quickly, rubbing the side of her arm, self-conscious. "I think I'd feel safer if you were closer."

"Oh," Jonathan said, two beats too late. Kate started to back into the bedroom again, waving her hands to dismiss her request.

"Never mind, it's okay, really," she said. "I can—"

Jonathan stood and started laughing. It stopped her words before they tripped off her tongue.

"Kate, it's okay," he said. "I don't mind in the least. Plus, this couch is really uncomfortable."

Kate felt her lips pull up at the corners. She'd bet that last part was for her benefit. The bodyguard moved toward her and she flipped the light back on so he could see the room. It was small and only housed a queen-size bed, a nightstand, a closet and a strip of carpet for limited foot traffic. Kate turned to see him sizing up the space and realized he might not have known what he was agreeing to do.

"There's nothing in here but the bed," she said, blunt. Jonathan let out another howl of laughter. Instead of backing out or teasing her, he kicked off his shoes and sat down on the side closest to the door. It sagged a bit beneath his weight as he lay down, so long his feet nearly went off the foot, and put his hands behind his head.

"If I turn the light off, won't it make you sleepy?" Kate asked, moving her hand over the switch. Jonathan shook his head. So she clicked it off and moved to the other side of the bed. If she hadn't been in her long T-shirt and pajama shorts, she wouldn't have suggested his supervision in the room. But, truth be told, she *did* need to get some sleep.

The bed dipped considerably less as she quickly shimmied under the displaced sheets and blanket. The bed might have been queen-size, but as she found the warm spot that her body had created before, she realized just how close the man next to her was. Although he was wearing the same shirt and pants from earlier that day and there was a swath of fabric between them, she could feel warmth from him seeping into her. It was more than just comforting.

Kate waited for her eyes to adjust to the darkness and the smallest ounce of light from the window while she rolled on her side and finally looked up at the man. Able to make out a wisp of his profile, she found her earlier thoughts on whatever moment they could have shared weighing on her just as heavily as her desire to save him the trouble of having her in his life. She pulled her hand out of the covers with the intention of taking his while the internal struggle between her happiness and his waged within her. Her hand paused in midair.

Do it, Kate.

But she couldn't. Her hand slid beneath her pillow.

"I'm sorry," she whispered into the dark. The sound of him moving his head toward her made the heat in her cheeks flare back to life.

"What for?"

Kate was sorry she'd been mean to him, callous and tactless about his profession when they'd met. She was sorry she'd been difficult and her singular focus had put him in danger. She was sorry that, despite the fact that he'd saved her at least three times, she didn't know how to really say thank-you. She was sorry for a lot of things, but couldn't find the words to connect that feeling to one thought.

"I'm not good with people," was all she said. In her mind it encompassed everything she felt guilty for right down to the moment she'd let slip away.

Jonathan moved some more, but in the darkness she couldn't pinpoint how.

"You're just fine for me."

Despite the lack of light, Jonathan's lips found hers with undeniable precision. Like his body, their warmth coaxed out a desire in Kate that she'd been trying to keep at bay. One that she felt growing stronger and stronger.

Jonathan broke the kiss and moved back.

"Sorry," he started, voice suddenly very low. "I—"

Kate pushed her body forward, hand out, taking

his face and bringing his lips back to hers. She'd interrupted him, but manners be damned. Jonathan's apology evaporated like the space between their two bodies. His lips were as hungry as hers, and soon their tongues joined each other in a tangled fray.

Kate moaned against him, against his taste. The sound seemed to charge the bodyguard even more. He rolled on top of her, elbows out to prop himself up, all without breaking their bond. Kate more than approved of the new position, putting her hands around his neck and pulling him down to her. For years, and maybe her entire life up until this point, she hadn't craved anyone as badly as she now craved this man. Kate moved her hands down to the bottom of his shirt and tugged upward with enthusiasm. Instead of it peeling off easily like she'd seen in countless movies, it stuck. Frustrated, she accidentally made a huff sound against his lips. She felt the same lips curve up into a smile. Jonathan broke their kiss, much to her dismay.

Without a word he sat up, now fully straddling her. Kate's chest heaved up and down, her face hot, but not as much as the rest of her when the bodyguard did something that really raised her temperature. With her eyes fully adjusted and able to make out what he was doing, Kate watched wide-eyed as the bodyguard pulled off his shirt and threw it on the floor. He lowered his lips back down to her, and instead of the hard crush of the last one, this kiss was a soft brush that left her wanting more. He moved his lips to her ear and whispered something that let Kate know exactly where she wanted this to go.

"Your turn."

LIKE LIGHTNING HAD struck her, Kate's eyelids flashed open. Something that had been hanging in the back of her mind was about to fall free. An idea, a theory on the tip of her tongue that bothered her on an almost emotional level. Something her mind was grasping for with such enthusiasm she'd woken up to help solve whatever problem it was attached to.

She started to get out of bed when an odd heaviness brought her attention to the man beside her, derailing her train of thought. Jonathan was on his side, fast asleep, his arm thrown over her—protective still. Kate smiled. She'd had a feeling the man had been just as tired as her.

Kate took a moment to watch the bodyguard sleep. In the soft light of early morning, she had an unobstructed view of his well-muscled chest with its light brushing of dark hair that slid down his stomach and disappeared beneath the sheets. She felt her cheeks heat with the knowledge of exactly what was beneath them. Despite her need to get some sleep, they'd spent quite a big portion of the rest of the night doing anything but.

She used all of her grace to move the man's arm off her and slip out of the bed without jostling him too much. He stirred but didn't wake up. Kate once again tiptoed across the room. Her body, she realized, was sore, but in a pleasant way. It reminded her of the way the bodyguard had felt with her. In every way. She smiled, still able to feel the impression of his lips against her skin.

Kate, as naked as the day she was born, collected her toiletries and clothes. She went into the badly tiled bathroom and showered quickly. Her mind had finally detached itself from the naked man in the room next door and focused on the feeling that was sticking out like a sore thumb in her mind. It felt like a hunch, but she didn't yet know what it was and why it was suddenly bothering her so much. Since she was positive she wasn't going to be able to fall back to sleep any time soon, she dressed in the clothes she'd packed for the convention without a second thought—a slightly sheer quarter-length sleeved burgundy blouse with a black camisole beneath that tucked right into wrinkle-free black slacks. Mind elsewhere still, she went through the motions of applying eyeliner, blush and dark red lipstick. She started to towel dry her hair when she remembered everything that had happened. Slowly she lowered the towel. Chances were attending the convention wouldn't be easy. It didn't seem like the couple was done yet, especially if they were working for anyone with half a brain. It wouldn't matter if they somehow were able to reverse engineer the drug. There wasn't enough time to do it before Kate presented her research.

She watched in the mirror as her expression hardened. She threw the towel over the shower rod and furiously brushed out her hair. When done, she gave herself one curt nod.

It was time to try to put an end to this.

Slipping into the flats she'd taken off in the living room, Kate padded to Jake's bedroom. To her surprise he still wasn't in the apartment, but then again, she knew that cases could often keep an agent away from home for days at a time. The larger room had a bed, desk and three waist-high filing cabinets. All with locks. Kate went to the one she'd jimmied open the night before—right before Jonathan had called her to dinner, noting she looked suspicious—and pulled it open. Jake had an office at the Bureau as well as one within Greg's lab. In both he had files and places to keep them safe. However, just as Jake had learned to become neat, he'd learned the importance of hard copies and backups. The filing cabinet she'd opened had information on dates and events that seemed to be tied to his job as Greg's handler. Most seemed to be written with code names, and as far as she could tell, there was no mention of the drug.

However, she had seen something the night before that was bothering her now. She shuffled through the files, trying to spark whatever trail she'd dismissed already. Minutes rolled by as she thumbed through and pulled out several different files.

What had she seen?

Frustrated, she turned and perched against the cabinet, trying to remember. Her eyes roamed the room around her as her mind went blank. She took in Jake's sparse bedroom decor—some knickknacks he'd saved through the years, pictures of trips he'd taken and memorabilia he'd collected and been given—when suddenly she knew exactly what it was she was looking for.

The theory that she had unconsciously formed even before waking became less of a *what if* and more of a terrifying possibility. With her stomach having dropped somewhere past her feet, she walked to one picture sitting on Jake's desk. Her hands trembled as she picked it up.

There it was.

It all made sense now.

Her phone buzzed in her pocket. She had been so focused on the picture that the motion startled her. She dropped the frame and winced as the glass cracked on impact.

Then she realized that was the least of her worries.

She fumbled for her phone and read Jake's ID flashing across the screen. Her stomach twisted.

"Jake," she started. But the man who responded definitely wasn't the boy she'd grown up with.

"No, but you can save him."

Chapter Twenty-One

Jonathan rolled onto his side, throwing his arm out so he wouldn't hit Kate. With his eyes still closed, he lowered it to the bed, careful he didn't hurt her.

But there was no Kate beneath it.

Jonathan opened one eye, took in the light from the window and looked at the empty spot next to him with a split feeling of warmth and coldness. Seeing where the scientist had been reminded him of what they had done, bringing a sense of unfamiliar happiness over him. At the same time, the empty spot highlighted the one fact that bodyguards needed to know at all times about their clients.

Where they were.

He swam his way out of the sheets and stopped when something fell to the floor. Confused, he bent over and picked up the book.

"Kate?" he called out into the apartment, pulling on his pants as he realized what he was holding. He opened the bedroom door and saw an empty kitchen and living space. Turning, he scanned the bathroom and found it, too, was empty. Cursing beneath his breath, he went for Jake's room.

Empty.

"Kate?" he called again, even though it was obvious she wasn't in the apartment. He ran to the front door, expecting there to be signs of a break-in. But there wasn't. Everything looked like it had after he'd locked them in the night before. The door's dead bolt was still thrown. Jonathan checked the windows next, but they, too, were locked.

"What's going on?" he asked the empty apartment.

Jonathan retrieved his phone and found no new calls or messages. He dialed Kate's number. It went straight to voice mail. The lack of ringing created an instant feeling of fear laced with panic. He looked down at the black book in his hand. Kate had left her notebook for him, he was sure, but why? And where was Jake? Had they gone somewhere together or had the agent not come home at all? He opened the notebook to the first page, hoping she'd left him some kind of clue.

He was disappointed. Kate's past five years of work were between his hands. Entrusted to him, but why?

Jonathan quickly dressed and decided to search the apartment for clues once more. All of Kate's things were still in the bedroom, but he noticed her toiletries had made it to the bathroom. There was also a wet towel. She'd showered. He moved on to the kitchen and living area, but nothing seemed to have changed from the night before. Lastly, he hit Jake's room, the least likely to hold any clue as to where the woman had gone, seemingly of her own accord.

Or was it?

One of the three filing cabinets beneath the window had a drawer pulled out. Even from the doorway he could see the lock had been broken. Jonathan walked over to inspect it when he noticed most of the papers were disheveled, like they'd been taken out one by one before being crammed back inside. *This* was what Kate had been up to before dinner.

Jonathan began to go through a few of the papers, trying to discern what Kate had been after, but without knowing Jake or Greg—whom the files mostly seemed to be about—he couldn't glean whatever Kate had. He slammed the drawer shut and was turning to leave when he spotted a picture lying upside down on the floor near the desk. Without much thought other than to put it back, he picked it up. Broken pieces of glass remained on the carpet. Curiosity piqued, he looked at the picture inside.

It wasn't a picture at all.

It was a letter.

A different kind of coldness came back.

Jonathan reached for his phone and scrolled through his pictures, stopping on the bloody letter left on Kate's hotel door. By the time he'd taken the picture, the words had been smeared by the blood. He opened his email and found Kate's Orion file. He pulled up the photocopies of every letter she'd received before she'd left Florida and scrolled through each. Halfway through he stopped. He didn't need to look any further to know the handwriting was a perfect match with the framed note in his hand.

"How could we have missed this?"

Anger seared through him as he quickly recalled the last three days with his new revelation. The one, he had no doubt, Kate had come to when she'd seen the note. How she must have felt, how she must have reacted, tore at a part of him he didn't even realize had been reserved just for thoughts of her. He put the frame down and was about to dial his boss's number. It was past time to loop her in. He needed help. However, his phone came to life instead. The number was unknown but he answered, cautious.

"Yes?"

"Mr. Carmichael?" Even though the man's voice was lowered, Jonathan was able to pick out who it belonged to easily enough.

"Jett?"

"Yeah, it's me. I thought you should know that man is back."

"Back? In the hotel?"

"I may have kept your and Miss Spears's reservations open in the computers," Jett quickly said. "I thought that it might help to keep you two hidden if they thought you were still here."

Jonathan could have kicked himself for not thinking of that before, just as he could have given the front desk attendant a huge bear hug right about then. This was exactly the break he needed.

"Jett, I need you to do me a huge favor," Jonathan said, already running into the living area to grab his keys. "Kate's gone and right now that man is the only lead I have to finding her. I need you to follow him, but don't say anything to him, and tell me where he's going. Can you do that?"

Jonathan shut the door behind him, not caring that he no longer had a way to get back inside. Kate had a key, and when he had Kate back it would all be okay.

"Jett?" he prodded after hesitation on the other end of the line continued.

"Yes, I can. I'll call you from the car."

KATE LOOKED OUT the window and down into the construction. The building next door was a few stories shorter and currently being built to match the one she was standing in. Though at a much slower pace.

"Progress isn't always as fast as we'd like it to be."

Kate turned in her leather chair and eyed the man who had been pulling the strings all along. A part of Kate withered at the sight of him. The other part flourished in anger.

"It all makes sense now," she said. "I guess the analytical part of me should be happy about that, at least." Kate laughed, a dry, quick sound. "From knowing what hotel I was staying at to knowing my plans while in New York." She laughed again, still as bitter as dark chocolate. "You knew everything, because we disclosed the information to you willingly."

Greg stood at the head of the table but didn't sit

down. He wore a dark brown suit with a spotted blue tie she'd actually bought him for his birthday a few years back. A bandage covered his right brow while cuts and swelling could be seen across the same side. He placed his hands on the top of the chair and squeezed the leather. He wasn't smiling, but he sure wasn't frowning, either. Either expression would have incited more anger on her part, but the blank look he was giving her was almost too much to bear. She fought the urge to look down at her hands.

"But how far down does the rabbit hole go, Greg? When did you become *this*? I don't even know how to describe you." Kate felt her eyes begin to water. She hoped she could keep it together long enough to at least understand *something*. "Why have you been terrorizing me—trying to kill me?" Her voice broke on the question and then nearly shattered on the next. "And where is Jake?"

Greg flexed his grip on the chair as if the motions helped him sort his thoughts. But Kate knew the man well enough—or at least she thought she had—to know it was a show. If Greg really had planned everything that happened so far, then he knew every reason why he'd done it without pausing.

"Do you remember when we first met, Kate? I believe you were eight. I asked you what you wanted to be when you were all grown up. Do you remember what you told me?"

Despite her desire to not play his game—whatever it was—Kate nodded.

"A dancer," she said.

Greg snapped his fingers.

"A dancer," he repeated. "Now, I have nothing against the performing arts or those who seek careers in its purview, but when I looked at you, saw how your mind worked, saw you talk and react to the world around you, I saw exactly what your mother did. I saw untapped potential coupled with an unquenchable curiosity. You didn't just question how the world worked, you tried to understand it. Seeing that raw innocence created within me a feeling of hope for the future so profound that I told you something I'd never told any other soul. Do you remember what that was?"

This time Kate didn't nod. She didn't have to sit there and tell him she remembered anything. They both knew she had never forgotten the words of a man her mother had once proclaimed was the smartest man she knew. Still, Greg waited a moment before continuing. He smiled as the words left his mouth.

"I told you that you were going to change the world." He let go of the chair top and clapped. "And by God, when you told me you'd had a breakthrough in your research, you proved that I was absolutely right!" His excitement began to ebb away, his smile falling slowly. He put his hands on the top of the chair again. Suddenly he looked tired. "I was so proud of you that, at first, I didn't realize what it meant. You, not even thirty, had found answers I hadn't yet been able to obtain despite my vast resources. In fact, your surprising achievements began to highlight my lack of them, showing my superiors that while I had the full force of the FBI behind me, all you had were two part-time lab techs who did menial work on something they had no idea was so important." One of his hands fisted. There was no trace of emotion besides a deep weariness that projected through the slight sagging of his face.

"Talk began to circulate about your achievement, about your work ethic, about your *potential*. For a while they praised me for finding you—for believing in you enough to challenge the Bureau to wait you out, to let you try to work out the solutions and not simply take them from you. That is, until their praise turned to anything but. Maybe I'd convinced them to wait for you because I didn't know how to do it myself. Maybe I had worked *so hard* to keep you associated with the project, without your knowledge, because I knew you wouldn't ask me to leave when *you* finally came on and took over. Maybe I was getting too old and a newer, brighter, younger face was needed." Kate watched as his expression burned white-hot with a flash of anger. It went out as fast as it had ignited. The extreme change in emotion seemed to leave him speechless for a moment. Kate capitalized on it.

"If I was out of the way, then you'd be able to keep your position, your lab and your reputation," she guessed. Even as he nodded, the child that had grown up looking to Greg as her role model tried to reason the admission away. He hadn't done anything. He couldn't have done anything. He was Greg.

But as his chin dipped down and then back up, the grown-up within Kate felt sick.

"I tried to warn you at first," he said. "And then scare you away."

"The notes," she said. It was the connection she'd made in Jake's room once she saw the handwritten letter Jake had received and framed when he graduated from the academy. It was handwriting she'd seen all her life and yet never thought about when staring at the same writing on the letters she'd received.

"I wanted to scare you away, make you realize that the spotlight should be put on someone more experienced."

"Like you."

"Yes, like me."

"But I didn't scare, did I?" she asked.

Greg's expression cracked again, showing another glimpse of anger she'd never seen from the man before.

"No, you didn't. Not even when a note found its way to your hotel-room door with real blood. You didn't even mention it to me the next day. So I had to escalate."

Kate didn't know what to do or say. The world she was currently sitting in didn't make sense. It was like she was back in her dream world. But this time Jonathan wasn't there to save her.

"You got that woman to try to run me over on the street," she breathed. "To just mow me down right in front of you. It was never about getting the case. It was about killing me."

"They don't call it an escalation for nothing," he said, almost teasing.

"But you were almost killed, too."

"That was truly an accident. One variable I didn't count on when we planned it was that Candice was harboring some fierce anger due to Donnie's impromptu knife show when he cut her arm to supply the blood found on the letter on your door." He dragged his finger up the inside of one of his arms. Finally she made the connection with the woman and the bandage. "I guess good help is hard to find sometimes, even from professionals. Her stress caused sloppiness that ended up working well for me in the end. Who would suspect me when I was so clearly a victim? Thankfully, I look much worse than I feel, and, luckily, not only did I have a backup plan, but Donnie was quick to employ it using a contact of his." The paramedic. He had been the backup plan. "But it still didn't work. No, there was another variable I hadn't accounted for."

"Jonathan." Just saying his name made a darkening world momentarily seem to lighten.

"I never thought you'd accept the help of a bodyguard, to be honest. Especially not one who would go above and beyond the scope of his job." He shook his head as if he was scolding her. "Breaking into the lab with Jake to save you was a big risk for him to take for someone he barely knew. Who really could have foreseen that happening?" He shook his head. "And just think, if Jonathan hadn't listened to you and saved you then, none of us would be in this situation we are in now."

Kate twisted her hands together in her lap.

"What have you done with Jake?" she whispered. Her trust in Greg was nothing compared to Jake's. While he'd become a mentor to her, Greg had become a father figure to her friend.

"Getting rid of Jake wouldn't benefit me or my plan. Being responsible for the death of an FBI agent—more specifically, my handler—would bring me unwanted attention. Not to mention, his affection for me keeps him from seeing exactly what I've done."

"He doesn't know you're behind all of this?" she asked, surprised.

Greg shook his head.

"His passion to avenge my pain and to keep you safe was getting him too close," he explained. "I sent Donnie to retrieve him yesterday. Once this is all over, Jake will be let go. No harm, no foul."

Kate was once again split between two emotions. Relief that Jake was okay and would be okay. Anger that Jake might never know the truth because of his love for the man standing near her.

"You betrayed us," Kate said. Adrenaline and tears made her voice tremble.

Greg nodded solemnly.

"I know your family has already felt this particular sting before, but just know it wasn't always part of the plan." He shrugged. "You simply forced my hand."

Chapter Twenty-Two

Kate's hands fisted. Was this what her mother had felt when she'd realized her team—the people she thought she knew better than anyone—had turned their backs on her?

"What now?" she asked instead. "If you wanted to simply kill me, why bring me here?"

Up until this point, Kate had almost been certain that Greg had needed to share his narrative with her. To explain why he was doing what he was doing. Whether it was cathartic or just a way for him to brag to someone, Kate didn't know. Either way, he answered her.

"I remembered your notebook. That intrepid little thing where you kept all of your notes written down, afraid that the world might take the ideas if they left the paper and ink of its pages. Knowing you, there's something in it that you've left out of the research you shared with me. Something I need to continue. And before you say you don't have it in New York, remember that I know you, Kate. I know you hid it in the hotel room just like I knew you would come here willingly to save Jake." Greg stepped up to the table. He lowered himself until he was pressing down on the glass top, a stance that showed he wanted her absolute full attention now. Not that he didn't already have it. "And once Donnie brings it to me, then I'll say goodbye."

Kate's mouth went dry.

"When they say never meet your idols, they weren't kidding," she whispered. Greg's lips pulled up at the corners.

"And when they said children were our future, how true that was, as well."

Kate watched as the man she had once loved like family turned his back on her. He walked to the door and knocked once before it opened, giving her a glimpse of the woman named Candice.

"No one comes in or out," he ordered. "And if she starts making too much noise, silence her."

Candice cast Kate a quick smirk.

"My pleasure."

Kate held her gaze, not wanting to back down until the door shut, leaving her alone inside. What had started out as a theory was now a full-blown walking nightmare. Not bringing the notebook had saved her life, at least temporarily, but now what if leaving it with Jonathan had endangered his?

Just because you're scared doesn't mean you're not strong.

Kate recalled her mother's words but, for once, found no comfort in them.

In that moment she felt nothing but weakness.

JONATHAN WAS STANDING across from yet another hotel, still in Manhattan but worlds different from where Jett worked.

"He went in there," Jett said, jogging up to Jonathan. He was still dressed in uniform but had taken his blazer off, draping it over his arm to look more casual. However, Jonathan looked up at the fifteen-story hotel and its glass-walled front and felt that maybe he was the one that looked too casual.

"Of course it is," he said. "This is where the convention is taking place in a few hours."

Jett joined his gaze and whistled.

"I applied for a job here once. It's a pretty fancy place. They have a glass atrium that makes you feel like you're not in a hotel at all."

"So, you've been in there before."

Jett nodded.

"Apparently I didn't have the right look, something about being too shaggy." He shrugged. "I've only seen the lobby, though, and not even for that long. They're pretty diligent about keeping nonguests out."

As soon as he'd been given the address of where Donnie had exited the cab, Jonathan had guessed simply walking in and asking if they'd seen Greg would have been frowned upon.

"So what's the plan?" Jett asked, gaze still turned to the hotel.

"You want to help us?" Jonathan asked, surprised. "Even though you have no idea what's going on?"

Jett shrugged again.

"If I did know, would that make Miss Spears in any less danger?"

Jonathan couldn't help but snort.

"No."

"Then, what's the plan?"

Jett followed along as Jonathan started for the nearest crosswalk and crossed the street. When they were near the double front doors, Jonathan spoke.

"Put this number in your cell phone." He recited the number when Jett's phone was out and made sure the man saved it. "I want you to call that number and tell the woman who answers that I told you to tell her something. Okay?" Jett nodded. "Tell her everything that has happened so far is because of Greg Calhoun. That he's trying to kill Kate and has been since we arrived. He's the one who sent her the letters, too." Jett's eyes widened, but he nodded again. "Tell her where we are and tell her I'm sorry I didn't tell her everything beforehand. Got that?"

"Yeah, when do you want me to do that?"

"Wait out here and give me five minutes and then call. I don't want to tip them off that I'm coming yet."

"And what are you going to do?"

Jonathan pulled out his wallet and counted out two hundred dollars in fifties and twenties.

"I'm going to go lie."

Like the outside, the inside was the complete opposite of the hotels Jonathan was used to. Not only was it as modern as they came—modular sofas and ottomans, white and gray everything with a smidgen of bright orange or blue and smooth, rounded front desks pushed to the side under the low part of the atrium—but as Jonathan walked across the gray tile, he was trying not to marvel at the giant art installations that could be seen from every floor, all the way up to the glass ceiling. It wasn't just a hotel. It was a destination.

He'd barely made it to one of the three front desks when a woman with the nameplate Julie chirped out a scripted welcome. It was all he could do to keep what he hoped was a pleasant and very innocent smile on his face.

"Actually, you can help me and a guest," he said, holding the money up. "I was getting into a taxi right outside when I noticed this lying in the backseat. The driver said it must have fallen out of one of your guests' pockets." Jonathan described the dark-haired man as if he'd heard a secondhand account from his made-up taxi driver. Even as he finished his description, her eyes widened in recognition.

"That sounds like Mr. Smith," she exclaimed. Jonathan wanted to roll his eyes at the name.

"Good! So you'll be able to return it to him," Jonathan said, mimicking her excitement. Julie nodded profusely, picking up the phone next to her. He fully intended to stall as long as he could, pretending to look at the art installations until he could see where Mr. Smith was going, when Julie decided to change the plan without even knowing it. She slid the money he'd put on the table back to him.

"I think Mr. Smith will want to thank you personally," she said after stepping aside to make the call. "It's not every day you find a less-than-greedy man. Most would have kept the money."

Jonathan shrugged.

"That just isn't my style."

Julie pointed out which elevator the man would most likely exit. Instead of skulking in the shadows trying to stalk him, Jonathan figured this bold approach worked just as well. Sooner or later he had bet he would come up against the man again.

Less than two minutes later, Jonathan watched as the elevator doors opened and none other than Mr. Smith was standing in front of him. His look of surprise was hidden quickly as Julie caught his eye and waved.

"I just wanted to return what you left behind," Jonathan said, voice dripping with fake cheer. He smiled for the benefit of Julie just as he suspected the man in front of him was doing.

"How thoughtful," he said, mouth stretched wide. He extended his hand and took the money before motioning for Jonathan to step inside. "To repay your kindness, how about we grab a drink upstairs?"

Jonathan kept smiling and got onto the elevator, now fully facing Julie's approving nod.

"Don't you think it's a little too early to drink?" Jonathan asked.

"Not when I'm celebrating."

The doors began to slide closed.

"And what's the occasion?" Jonathan asked. His entire body tensed as the man pressed the button for the second floor from the top.

"I was about to leave to finish a job," the man said, moving back to his spot against the elevator wall. The elevator doors shut as soon as he finished his next thought. "But it appears that now I don't have to leave at all."

The man reached in his blazer and pulled out a knife just as Jonathan turned and hiked his foot up. He pushed the man away from him just as Mr. Smith swiped at his shin. The knife sliced his pants but didn't cut deeper. Had he not reacted as fast as he did, Jonathan knew that wouldn't have been the case.

Mr. Smith turned the hilt of his knife so he was holding the blade down, arcing it through the air in between them with force. Jonathan lunged forward, grabbing for the man's wrist. He caught it as the man pulled it up, ready for another swipe. Jonathan used his free hand to send a punch against the man's face, but he moved out of range too quickly. The jolt loosened Jonathan's hold on his wrist and he had to jump back, hitting the elevator wall so hard that it shook, to avoid the knife's curved, sharp blade.

Jonathan pushed off the wall, knowing the man wouldn't stop until he had gutted him in the elevator, and grabbed for his arm again. This time, though, he wasn't lucky. The tip of the knife came down before he could push Mr. Smith's arm out of the way. The blade moved across Jonathan's forearm, cutting through his long-sleeve button-up as well as his skin. He made a grunt as the pain registered, but knew the cut hadn't been a direct hit. He pivoted back, moving his left side away from another attack and used the momentum to bring up his right elbow. It connected with the side of the man's nose in a sickening crack and then a spray of blood.

The man let out a howl and swung around in an angry spiral. Once again the knife connected with Jonathan's skin—this time his shoulder.

Jonathan felt the warm liquid before he saw the blood seeping through his shirt. The elevator began to slow and Jonathan just hoped the doors would open soon.

"Fighting an unarmed man seems cowardly." He grabbed his shoulder and moved to the corner. Mr. Smith was also in pain. All humor he'd once had seemed to have broken along with his nose. He held the knife out and wiped the blood from his nose with the back of his other hand. It did nothing but smear the red around.

"Where's the notebook?" he bit out.

"Where's Kate?" Jonathan bit right back.

It angered the man more than the nose break seemed to and he lashed out in another burst of fury just as the elevator doors opened. Without time to glance back to see where he was running out into, Jonathan backed out of the small space and into a much more expansive one. From his periphery he saw more modular couches and closed doors on either side of him. He didn't have time to investigate further.

Mr. Smith wasn't done with him yet.

KATE HADN'T BEEN blindfolded when she was brought into the hotel or the small yet lavish boardroom she was currently being held in. She had given Jonathan her notebook, called a taxi, walked into the lobby and told the front desk attendant she was expected. Then Kate had taken the elevator to the fourteenth floor and walked right into the same boardroom, all without hesitation, to wait for Greg to show up and tell her of her and Jake's fates.

It had been easy to get there.

But she now expected it would be exponentially harder to leave.

She rapped her knuckles against the door and stepped all the way back to the table, trying to show that she in no way meant trouble.

The door opened slowly until the woman's annoyance was seen clearly on her expression. She sized Kate up.

"I just want to talk," Kate pleaded.

Candice snorted, not interested.

"Then talk," she said. Kate took a tentative step forward.

"Do you know who Greg Calhoun really is?" she asked. Candice, an exceptionally pretty woman when she wasn't trying to murder people, paused but didn't release the door handle. "Do you know who he works for?"

"If the money's good, I don't need to know," Candice said.

"He works for the FBI," Kate added quickly. Candice didn't move from her spot, but she did roll her eyes.

"So?"

"So, did he even tell you his plan? His endgame? Or does enough money mean you don't care about going to prison?"

Candice's eye actually spasmed, a quick pulse of hidden emotion breaking through. Once again she didn't move.

"Greg is a scientist. He wants me out of the way so he can take over my work—my research—and continue to work with the FBI after I'm dead. Did you know that?" Kate knew the woman didn't. Her lips had pursed. "My mother was FBI, my friend that Donnie took is FBI and for the last five years I've been under FBI monitoring. Don't you think if I show up dead, not to mention my friend being kidnapped, that an investigation is going to be opened? And if Greg plans to keep his job, then surely he's going to need one strong alibi or one heck of a fall guy…or woman. That case you two stole was given to me by Greg—why do you think he had you steal it back if not to help frame you?" Kate paused for dramatic effect. She noticed Candice's hand had curled into a small fist.

"Listen," Kate began again. "I've known Greg almost all of my life. He's been my role model since I was a little girl. Now he's trying to destroy what I hoped would be my life's work and, well, me. If he's willing to kill someone he once claimed to love like a daughter, do you think for one second he'd hesitate to throw you and your partner under the bus?"

Candice put her back against the door, holding it open still, and crossed her arms over her chest.

"So, what? I should go ahead and kill all of you?" she asked, sarcasm rampant. Kate didn't back down.

"You'd be hunted hard and you know that."

The woman narrowed her eyes.

"If you want my opinion, and I should point out that the FBI wants me for my intelligence, if I was you I would run now. Before all of this gets resolved, you could be out of the state," Kate said. "I'll make sure it's known that you let me go, so if you ever get caught, then you'll look a lot better than if you shot a defenseless woman point-blank. What do you say?"

Chapter Twenty-Three

Jonathan ducked Mr. Smith's next swing. This time he was able to use his right arm to hook the crazed man's arm in a viselike grip. Jonathan squeezed. The hold intensified until the man yelled. The sweet sound of the knife falling to the ground met Jonathan's ears. Mr. Smith wasn't as much of a fan. He used his other hand, fisting it, and delivered a blow to Jonathan's temple that utterly dazed him. He released the man and staggered to the side.

But not before kicking the fallen knife backward as hard as he could.

"You are a pain he didn't warn us about," the man said, half bent, hand to his nose. Jonathan's vision started to fringe black as he went to the closest wall and put his hand against it to try to steady not only his balance but everything else. Jonathan blinked several times, trying to keep from passing out, until the feeling subsided. He pushed off the wall and started to run for the man again. He knew he needed to level the playing field before another player was added to the game. This man might have a knife, but he knew for a fact that his female partner had a gun.

Mr. Smith had no choice but to take Jonathan's shoulder in the chest. He staggered backward but grabbed hold of Jonathan's sleeve to keep from falling. It tugged the man down enough that he got an un-inhibited view of something that made his blood run cold despite the exertion they were putting out.

The man used Jonathan's momentary distraction to his advantage. He brought his hand up and pressed hard into the gash in Jonathan's shoulder. Unlike the one in his forearm, this wound was deeper and much more painful. Jonathan once again found himself backing away, fighting a new wave of pain.

"I see you got a good look at my collection," Mr. Smith said, nearly out of breath. He motioned to the inside of his blazer before opening both sides. Jonathan eyed them with an expanding feeling of unease. Attached inside were at least ten knives, ranging in size. "They're beautiful, aren't they?" The man leaned on the wall behind him. He was stalling. "Most people like guns, but me? Well, these are just so much more poetic, don't you think?"

Jonathan didn't pay attention to what the two knives the man pulled out looked like. He knew they would hurt no matter their decoration or size. Instead he ran back toward the elevator, then cut into the small lounge area set up in the corner. While he wished he knew exactly where the Taser was that he'd given to Kate, he spotted the only thing that might give him a small chance to defend himself. Jonathan hoisted the closed umbrella out of the concrete cylinder and brandished it like a sword, wishing again that he'd brought a gun with him to the city. Or at least had had the sense to calm down enough to grab the Taser from his bag before coming to the hotel.

Mr. Smith was nearly on him, like a bull drawn to a matador. In one hand he had a new knife turned downward, reminiscent of a bad guy in a slasher movie, while the other was held up and out, easier for quick jabs. Jonathan quickly judged the surroundings of the small lounge, the elevators to the left and the hall leading to what must have been a corporate meeting floor, and realized he was in the worst possible corner. There was no way to move around the raging, bloodied man.

So Jonathan decided to go through him.

He opened the umbrella wide and rammed it into the man's chest. Using his momentum, he carried the man backward to the far wall before he was able to slice through the material. Jonathan tried to pull the umbrella back so he could use it as a bat, but Mr. Smith's knives got too close again. One went through the fabric and moved through Jonathan's shirt and skin with ease. The umbrella fell between them. Jonathan tried to back away again, but Mr. Smith was quick. He stretched out his leg and tripped Jonathan, sending the man to fall hard without any time to catch himself.

"Like I said," Mr. Smith said, a wild smile pulling up his bloodstained lips, "a pain in my si—"

A gunshot exploded in the hallway.

Jonathan cringed, waiting for the pain. However, it didn't come. It was Mr. Smith who seemed to have taken the bullet. He tipped over and hit the floor in a spray of blood. He'd been shot in the head.

Jonathan turned, confused, to see the dark blond-haired woman lowering her gun in the middle of the hallway.

"Jonathan!"

Farther back, turning the corner, was Kate. She was the most beautiful woman he'd ever seen. The woman between them, however, pulled his attention back. She met his gaze with a smirk and put the gun in the back of her pants.

Jonathan stood as she walked closer and bent over the man.

"That's for slicing me open," she growled. Some other not-so-nice words were said before Kate was at Jonathan's side.

"You're hurt," she exclaimed, already touching his newest cut on his upper arm.

"You should see the other guy."

The woman straightened and snorted at that. Jonathan was ready to fight her for her gun when she turned to Kate.

"Donnie has a suite on the next floor," she said. "That's where your friend is. Use this in the elevator to get there." The woman pulled a gold key card from her back pocket. Kate took it with a nod and looked down at the dead man on the ground. It definitely wasn't a good scene. "If it makes you feel better, even by my standards he was a very, very bad man." As if to emphasize her dislike for him, Candice gave him one swift kick to the ribs.

Kate didn't comment. Jonathan took her hand and pulled her a few feet to the elevator.

"Don't worry," Kate whispered as the doors shut. "She can run, but she can't hide forever."

"I guess telling you we should go get help first wouldn't work," Jonathan said. Kate was already holding the key card up to where she needed to swipe it through.

"Greg doesn't want Jake to know he's involved. I'm assuming Greg will use everything in his power to pin it all on Candice and her partner. Since Jake trusts Greg as much as I once did, that might be easier than it would have been otherwise. I doubt Greg is anywhere near Jake right now," she reasoned. "Plus…" She swiped the card and slowly they began to ascend to the next floor. "I'm not leaving him behind."

"I wouldn't ask you to," Jonathan replied, taking her hand. As far as he could tell, she seemed okay physically. Mentally—emotionally—he'd bet Greg's betrayal would leave a wound that might never heal. But Kate was strong. She would survive this like she'd survived everything else.

THE ELEVATOR DOORS slid open to show an entryway that was the very definition of opulent. Shiny surfaces, detailed decor and modern everything else set the tone for an obviously expensive stay. Kate wondered how a man like Donnie afforded such a place, but then stopped that thought. If Greg had offered them enough money so they didn't ask any questions—and didn't *want* to— she'd bet the man had done similar jobs beforehand, making a penthouse a much more affordable option.

Jonathan, bleeding but standing tall, kept hold of her hand. He didn't ask her why she hadn't woken him before leaving for the hotel, and, in a way, she'd bet he already knew it was to keep him safe. He moved out of the elevator and angled himself so if anyone were to jump out at them, he'd take the brunt of it. She squeezed his hand, hoping he knew how much she appreciated it.

They stepped out of the entryway and right up to a city view that probably made the penthouse as expensive as she imagined it was. Windows that were used as walls stretched to the left, running along a living space, dining and bar area, before dipping out of view into what must have been the kitchen. Off the living area was a hallway that led to the bedrooms. They looked in each massive and lavishly decorated room one by one until they had only the biggest bedroom and its bathroom left.

Kate's palms began to sweat. What if Candice had lied? What if Greg had? What if they'd killed Jake the day before and she'd come voluntarily to exchange her life for his for no reason at all?

"I can't," Kate said, pulling back when they neared the bathroom door. There was nowhere else he could be. Jonathan caught her off guard by turning her so quickly she nearly stumbled and kissing her full on the lips. It was hard and powerful.

"You can," he said after they broke apart. "I'm right here with you."

And that was all she needed to hear.

Stepping forward, she opened the door and didn't hesitate walking inside. The bathroom, like its connected bedroom, was massive and beautiful. A marbled vanity, a walk-in shower that looked like it could fit at a least ten people and a Jacuzzi tub with an FBI agent inside.

"Jake!"

Kate and Jonathan rushed over to the man, whose arms, legs, hands and feet were bound by rope and his mouth covered with tape. For one wild moment Kate felt like she was back in that warehouse all those years ago. Instead of her mother, it was her best friend.

"He's breathing," Jonathan said, cutting through the bad memory. She shook her head. She needed to focus on the here and now.

"Jake? Can you hear me?" Kate asked. She put her fingers against his pulse and sighed in relief. It wasn't strong, but it didn't seem to be too weak, either.

"I think he was knocked unconscious at some point." Jonathan pointed to the agent's forehead. Dried blood plastered some of his fair hair against his scalp.

Kate bent over and ripped the tape off his mouth. Jonathan undid his hands and started on the arms when a voice paused both of their hands.

"Step away from him."

Kate turned to find Greg standing in the doorway, a gun angled at the space between them.

"Greg," Jonathan started, moving slowly out of the tub and in front of Kate, "let's talk about this."

Greg, who had been the picture of calculated calm earlier, had noticeably changed. His demeanor was slightly rumpled, carrying through his clothes and right down to the crease between his brows. He pushed his glasses up the bridge of his nose, hindered a bit by the bandage, but didn't drop the aim of his gun, instead moving it to Kate herself.

"Let's go have a talk," he said, voice nearly a whisper. "Now, or I'll shoot all three of you."

Jonathan gave Kate a look that quite clearly seemed to say he would take out the man if he could, but she had already judged the distance between Greg's gun and them. He'd be able to get at least one shot off before Jonathan could make a move.

"Okay, we'll come," Kate said, for everyone's benefit.

Greg nodded and began to back out into the bedroom. As if he was pulling on an invisible thread, Jonathan walked with matching speed. Kate followed, but before she cleared the bathroom door, she paused and looked back at her best friend. When he woke up the world would be much different. She only hoped he'd figure out what happened.

As if her intense worry could be heard, Jake's eyes flashed open. It took everything she had not to give away her relief. The other two men were out of his sight line. Kate hoped he wouldn't call out to her, to let Greg know he was conscious, so then Greg would be forced to silence him, too. However, he kept quiet and even lifted one finger to his lips to silence her.

Kate gave a quick nod and turned back to Greg. She stuck her hand in Jonathan's and they were led back to the living area.

"Backs to the window," Greg ordered, rotating around them so Jonathan was never in range to do anything about the gun pointed at them. Kate squeezed his hand, hoping he'd somehow understand that Jake wasn't down and out for the count. "I *knew* you wouldn't be easy," Greg said when they were in position. While Jonathan had once again positioned himself as a human shield, Kate moved so their shoulders were touching. She was going to face the man. "Within the span of, what, less than an hour, you two have managed to turn everything on its head."

"Or maybe it was just a bad plan," Jonathan said, anger clear. His shoulders were as straight as an arrow, his body tense.

"You have to know the authorities are on their way," Kate pointed out. "Someone must have heard the shot downstairs."

Greg snorted.

"I know they are," he said, an easy smile lifting the corner of his lips. "You two may have been a pain, but you've actually helped me more than you know." Kate raised her eyebrow, questioning. "My two scapegoats look even more guilty than they did before. One obviously used force against you," he said, motioning to Jonathan's cuts, "and the other fled, further proving that's she's just as guilty." Jonathan squeezed her hand several times. Kate's confusion at the pressure diminished when she saw Jake walking along the hallway behind Greg. He was limping, but not enough that it made noise. Still, Kate wanted to keep talking just in case.

"So you're going to just kill us and then what?" Kate asked, anger mounting. "Call the cops and pretend you found us and Jake? Do you think they're really going to believe it all? And, while we're at it, do you think the FBI will really let you take over my work? Surely you've thought about this objectively and seen that if I could figure out it was you behind this based on a handwritten letter, the Bureau could also piece it together."

Kate was trying to keep her eyes off Jake as he got closer, but she had a feeling Jonathan knew exactly what was going on. He applied pressure to her hand again before letting go completely. Whatever was going to happen was about to take place.

"You may be one smart cookie, Kate," Greg said, "but that doesn't mean I'm not, also." He raised the gun and then the world went chaotic.

Jake tackled Greg to the side just as the gun discharged. Kate braced for the hit but was instead thrown to the side, as well. Jonathan's weight sandwiched her to the ground and covered her as the window behind them shattered. Kate closed her eyes tight and waited for the world to quiet.

"Are you okay?"

Kate looked up at the bodyguard and blinked several times.

"Kate?" he prodded, his hand cupping her cheek. They were still on the ground, the sound of the wind roaring past the newly opened window almost carrying his words away.

"Yeah, I think so," she said, quickly cataloging any new pain. Aside from the fall, there wasn't any. "What about you?"

Jonathan got up and nodded as an answer, but moved away quickly, running over to Jake and Greg. Kate scrambled to her feet and followed.

"Oh, my God," Kate breathed.

Jake had managed to push the man to the ground and take possession of his gun, but it was how he'd disabled him that floored her. Greg was sitting up, back leaning against the couch, grabbing his neck. In Jake's other hand was an automated injector.

Empty.

"You injected him with the prototype," she said, not a question.

Jonathan helped the agent to his feet. He nodded.

"I found it in the bedroom. Had to improvise."

Greg looked between them with wide eyes behind his glasses. He looked so helpless without a weapon, without his banter, that a younger Kate would have felt sorry for him. However, now all she felt was a sense of loss.

Kneeling down, she looked him square in the eye.

"Congratulations, Greg," she said. "You just became the first human trial."

Chapter Twenty-Four

"How did you figure it out?" Kate asked. She and Jake sat at what was no doubt a very expensive table in the penthouse as cops swarmed the space. Soon they'd be called off. Jake's boss was on the way.

"I didn't," he answered honestly. "At least not until I came to in the bathroom."

"But he told me you were getting too close," Kate said, confused. "That's why he got Donnie to grab you."

Jake's jaw tensed.

"He was wrong. I was still looking into Donnie's identity as well as that Candice woman's when he jumped me near my apartment." Jake fisted his hand on top of the table. When he met Kate's eyes, there was an immense weight there. One she knew all too well. "The thing is, I never suspected him, Kate. I never once thought Greg could be behind it all. And you and Jonathan were almost killed because of it."

Kate put her hand on his. It was the same show of affection she'd given to the bodyguard, but it was completely different at the same time. Her feelings for Jake had, and would always be, that of an almost sibling type of love. Jonathan, on the other hand…

"Being blinded by love isn't something to apologize for," she said. "Greg knows us as well as our parents. He knew how to work us, how to move the pieces around so we wouldn't suspect him. He used our love for him to his cruel advantage, and that wasn't something either one of us saw coming." She patted his hand and Jake gave a little nod. Although he knew the truth in her words, she knew it would be a long time before he forgave himself.

"I guess your dad really saved the day," he said after a moment. He motioned to Jonathan off to the side, talking to Jett, which had been a surprise in itself, and the paramedic who was bandaging his cuts. Luckily, none were serious. The bodyguard looked over to Kate and she gave him a quick smile. "If Jonathan hadn't been around…"

He didn't need to finish the thought. Kate didn't, either. She knew she owed the dark-haired man her life, many times over.

Jake's boss, a woman named Melanie who looked as if she'd just stepped out of a catalog titled something like Those Who Don't Put Up With Any Nonsense, showed up a few minutes later. She was happy that Jake and Kate were all right, but the anger that she too had been hoodwinked by Greg covered her relief quickly. Jonathan joined Kate as they recounted everything that had happened while Jake was sent to the hospital to get his head wound checked out.

"What will happen to Greg?" Kate asked when they were done. He'd been conscious but unresponsive by the time the cops had come and taken him out of the penthouse, despite Kate's protests. When the FBI had come in, they had collected him and taken him to the hospital. "That stage of the drug hasn't been tested. If its results are like the earlier one, then there's only a limited amount of time in which we can help him. Though, to be honest, unless he has an antidote already created, I probably won't have the time."

Melanie uncrossed her legs. She looked to Jonathan and asked if he'd excuse the two of them. He nodded and returned to Jett, who'd been sidelined by another agent. His involvement had touched Kate, being a stranger but still willing to help. Despite everything that had happened, his hotel would be getting a perfect review from her.

"Kathryn, I understand if you're not that happy with us and the decisions we've made in the past few years in regards to your work," Melanie said, voice all business. "But the goal of this convention was always to offer you a position. One that would consist of your own lab, a team of bright minds to help you and close to unlimited funding and resources. I know getting to this spot took a very different route than either of us anticipated, but this offer is now officially on the table." She pressed her fingertip to the table between them, physically underlining her point. Kate watched the show with little conflict. While she hadn't liked the way they'd gone about it, in the end she trusted Jake's love of where he worked. Just as her mother had.

Betrayal, danger and loss couldn't always be accounted for, but Kate knew that in her line of work the chances of falling into any of them were great. That wouldn't stop her, though.

Instead of giving the answer she knew she always would have given—yes—Kate looked over at Jonathan. What she believed would have been an easy answer suddenly didn't feel that way.

"Looks like you got me to the convention after all, Mr. Bodyguard," Kate said, finally able to have a moment alone with him. They'd been asked to leave the penthouse and were now in the corner of the lobby while all sorts of uniforms bustled about. "One heck of a last field assignment, too."

Jonathan smiled.

"What can I say?" he teased. "I'm just that good."

Kate's smile lit up her entire body, highlighting a nothing short of amazing woman. When that smile began to fade, Jonathan already knew what would happen next.

"They offered you the job," he said, making sure to keep a smile on his face and in his voice.

Kate nodded.

"Apparently Greg is sitting in the hospital right now answering every question he's asked," she said. "I don't know how anyone else will react to the untested drug, but for now we know it works in part."

"That's great," he said honestly.

"They want to go ahead and fly me home to collect my research and come straight back to sift through Greg's." A small blush reddened her cheeks. "It's all happening so fast."

Jonathan didn't have to fake the smile anymore. He was truly happy for her.

"So what happens now?" she asked after a moment of silence passed between them. Her dark eyes searched his face, looking for something he wasn't sure he had. Kate's potential—her dream—was finally being fully realized. Her life was about to change in the best way possible. Even though he wanted more than anything to see that happen, Jonathan knew he wouldn't be a part of it. She was way above his level, and he realized with a drop of his stomach that he'd known that since the moment he'd met her.

"Well, the contract is fulfilled," he said. "I'll return to Dallas and finally get the desk job I always wanted, and you—" He paused, a swell of longing almost making him reach forward and pull her into an embrace she wouldn't forget. "And you, Miss Scientist, will continue trying to save the world."

"I'M GLAD YOU didn't get sick."

Jonathan turned and smiled up at his boss. Nikki was dressed in a long gown, a deep gray a shade darker than the maid of honor's dress. The soft thumping of an

'80s throwback had guests and the man and woman of the hour dancing a few feet from his table.

"To be honest, there was a moment I was worried I would," he said. "But then I thought about all of the flack I'd catch from Mark, Oliver and you and knew I needed to keep it together." Nikki laughed and leaned against the empty chair next to him.

"Well, I'll tell you, it was a hilarious, heartfelt best man speech," she said. "I think you almost made Mark cry."

Jonathan couldn't help but laugh at that thought.

It had been two months since he'd returned from New York. Two months since he'd seen or heard from Kate. Since then, Nikki had stayed true to her word and offered him a job that kept him in one place—though, instead of sitting at a desk, he was now the new trainer and recruiter for Orion. Interacting with and vetting current and potential agents was a job he was starting to find he really enjoyed—even though he was surprised Nikki hadn't fired him on the spot when she learned the extent of the events that had happened in New York, and that he'd kept them a secret from her until they'd been resolved.

Then again, he wasn't really that surprised, either.

At the end of the day, Nikki was one of his best friends.

"Well, look at what we have here." Jonathan turned this time to see Oliver Quinn and his wife, Darling, walk up. Oliver was wearing a copy of the tuxes Mark and Jonathan had on while his wife wore a slightly different version of Nikki's dress—one that had had to be modified for her large pregnant belly. "Jonathan and Nikki, the only people *not* dancing." Oliver turned to his wife and smirked. "Why don't we show them how it's done?"

Darling laughed as Oliver held out his hand to Nikki. Jonathan, already knowing his fate, jumped up and extended his hand to Darling, smiling.

"Don't worry," she said as they shuffled onto the dance floor. "All I can really do is sway back and forth."

Jonathan laughed and together they began to move to the beat. He enjoyed the dance and their talk about a case she had just finished working, names redacted, of course, but something inside still didn't feel quite right. Sure, he was surrounded by his closest friends— his family, really—and all of their loved ones and the happiness that seemed to be contagious, but there was something missing. Well, someone.

"Excuse me," a voice said from behind him, "but can I have this dance?"

Darling looked at the woman who cut into their swaying with an all-knowing smile. She gave Jonathan, who had frozen altogether, a wink.

"I'd love that," she said, before backing up to where her husband and Nikki looked on with smiles.

Jonathan turned to the woman and couldn't believe his eyes.

"Kate?"

Kate Spears was wearing a long light blue dress, had her hair curled to her shoulders and had a small, shy smile across her perfect lips. She took one of his hands and placed the other on her hip.

"I'm also a fan of just swaying, if that's okay with you," she said.

Jonathan felt himself nod, absolutely confused. He cast another quick look at his friends to see Mark and his new bride, Kelli, giving him the thumbs-up.

"How are you here?"

Kate gave a tiny laugh that made Jonathan smile instantly. They began to sway to the beat as she answered.

"Well, a man named Mark tracked me down and said this wedding was the place to be. That *everyone* who was anyone would be here." She shrugged. "I decided my handler and I needed a break after all the work we've done the last two months." She glanced off to the side and Jonathan caught sight of Jake, also dressed up, talking to one of the guests, an attractive young woman from Mark's family.

"That makes sense," he said, attention falling back squarely on her. The music could have stopped right then and he wouldn't have noticed. "How is all that going?"

"Interestingly. I consolidated my old lab as well as Greg's and was even able to pick my colleagues. They don't seem to be against my age, which is nice. Did you hear about Candice?"

Jonathan nodded.

"Nikki told me she was caught trying to flee to Mexico."

"Accurate. Now, like Greg, she's answering for her crimes."

Jonathan didn't pry beyond what he was given when it came to Greg. Even now when she mentioned him he could tell it hurt. He let them sway a moment longer before pressing on.

"So, you're living in New York now?"

Kate's cheeks reddened slightly.

"Actually, that's one thing I wanted to talk to you about," she said. "I was hoping you could help us find some good apartments. We're currently staying at a hotel not too far from here, but I don't need to tell you how much I've come to dislike hotels."

Jonathan was afraid he'd heard incorrectly. He almost didn't want to ask and be corrected, but his curiosity got the better of him.

"Wait, you want to get an apartment here in Dallas?"

Kate's cheeks turned a darker shade, but she kept smiling all the same.

"Considering I got my lab moved here, I thought that might be a good idea."

Jonathan felt that missing piece finally fall into place. A smile as true as they came graced his lips. He pulled Kate closer.

"I think I could help with that," he said. He twirled her around before bringing her back into his embrace. She let out a stream of laughter.

"Who knew you could dance, Mr. Bodyguard," she said.

"I just needed the right partner, Miss Scientist."

Together they continued to dance, even as the slow song ended. With a quick look around the dance floor,

Jonathan realized he was surrounded by his friends, their families and a woman who made the smile on his face reach all the way down to his heart.

With one thought, he felt a contentment he'd always wanted but never thought possible.

Roots.

* * * * *

Tyler Anne Snell's ORION SECURITY
miniseries concludes next month with
SUSPICIOUS ACTIVITIES.
Look for it wherever
Harlequin Intrigue books are sold!

THE MONTANA HAMILTONS *Series*
by B.J. Daniels goes on.
Turn the page for a sneak peek at INTO DUST...

CHAPTER ONE

THE CEMETERY SEEMED unusually quiet. Jack Durand paused on the narrow walkway to glance toward the Houston skyline. He never came to Houston without stopping by his mother's grave. He liked to think of his mother here in this beautiful, peaceful place. And he always brought flowers. Today he'd brought her favorite: daisies.

He breathed in the sweet scent of freshly mown lawn as he moved through shafts of sunlight fingering their way down through the huge oak trees. Long shadows fell across the path, offering a breath of cooler air. Fortunately, the summer day wasn't hot and the walk felt good after the long drive in from the ranch.

The silent gravestones and statues gleamed in the sun. His favorites were the angels. He liked the idea of all the angels here watching over his mother, he thought, as he passed the small lake ringed with trees and followed the wide bend of Braes Bayou situated along one side of the property. A flock of ducks took flight, flapping wildly and sending water droplets into the air.

He'd taken the long way because he needed to relax. He knew it was silly, but he didn't want to visit his mother upset. He'd promised her on her deathbed that he would try harder to get along with his father.

Ahead, he saw movement near his mother's grave and slowed. A man wearing a dark suit stood next to the angel statue that watched over her final resting place. The man wasn't looking at the grave or the angel. Instead, he appeared to simply be waiting impatiently. As he turned…

With a start, Jack recognized his father.

He thought he had to be mistaken at first. Tom Durand had made a point of telling him he would be in Los Angeles the next few days. Had his father's plans changed? Surely he would have no reason to lie about it.

Until recently, that his father might have lied would never have occurred to him. But things had been strained between them since Jack had told him he wouldn't be taking over the family business.

It wasn't just seeing his father here when he should have been in Los Angeles. It was seeing him in this cemetery. He knew for a fact that his father hadn't been here since the funeral.

"I don't like cemeteries," he'd told his son when Jack had asked why he didn't visit his dead wife. "Anyway, what's the point? She's gone."

Jack felt close to his mother near her grave. "It's a sign of respect."

His father had shaken his head, clearly displeased with the conversation. "We all mourn in our own ways. I like to remember your mother my own way, so lay off, okay?"

So why the change of heart? Not that Jack wasn't glad to see it. He knew that his parents had loved each other. Kate Durand had been sweet and loving, the perfect match for Tom, who was a distant workaholic.

Jack was debating joining him or leaving him to have this time alone with his wife, when he saw another man approaching his father. He quickly stepped behind a monument. Jack was far enough away that he didn't recognize the man right away. But while he couldn't see the man's face clearly from this distance, he recognized the man's limp.

Jack had seen him coming out of the family import/export business office one night after hours. He'd asked his father about him and been told Ed Urdahl worked on the docks.

Now he frowned as he considered why either of the men was here. His father hadn't looked at his wife's grave even once. Instead he seemed to be in the middle of an intense conversation with Ed. The conversation ended abruptly when his father reached into his jacket pocket and pulled out a thick envelope and handed it to the man.

He watched in astonishment as Ed pulled a wad of money from the envelope and proceeded to count it.

Even from where he stood, Jack could tell that the gesture irritated his father. Tom Durand expected everyone to take what he said or did as the gospel.

Ed finished counting the money, put it back in the envelope and stuffed it into his jacket pocket. His father seemed to be giving Ed orders. Then looking around as if worried they might have been seen, Tom Durand turned and walked away toward an exit on the other side of the cemetery—the one farthest from the reception building. He didn't even give a backward glance to his wife's grave. Nor had he left any flowers for her. Clearly, his reason for being here had nothing to do with Kate Durand.

Jack was too stunned to move for a moment. What had that exchange been about? Nothing legal, he thought. A hard knot formed in his stomach. What was his father involved in?

He noticed that Ed was heading in an entirely different direction. Impulsively, he began to follow him, worrying about what his father had paid the man to do.

Ed headed for a dark green car parked in the lot near where Jack himself had parked earlier. Jack dropped the daisies, exited the cemetery yards behind him and headed to his ranch pickup. Once behind the wheel, he followed as Ed left the cemetery.

Staying a few cars back, he tailed the man, all the time trying to convince himself that there was a rational explanation for the strange meeting in the cemetery or his father giving this man so much money.

But it just didn't wash. His father hadn't been there to visit his dead wife. So what was Tom Durand up to?

Jack realized that Ed was headed for an older part of Houston that had been gentrified in recent years. A row of brownstones ran along a street shaded in trees. Small cafes and quaint shops were interspersed with the brownstones. Because it was late afternoon, the street wasn't busy.

Ed pulled over, parked and cut his engine. Jack turned into a space a few cars back, noticing that Ed still hadn't gotten out.

Had he spotted the tail? Jack waited, half expecting Ed to emerge and come stalking toward his truck. And what? Beat him up? Call his father?

So far all Ed had done from what Jack could tell was sit and watch a brownstone across the street.

Jack continued to observe the green car, wondering how long he was going to sit here waiting for something to happen. This was crazy. He had no idea what had transpired at the cemetery. While the transaction had looked suspicious, maybe his father had really been visiting his mother's grave and told Ed to meet him there so he could pay him money he owed him. But for what that required such a large amount of cash? And why in the cemetery?

Even as Jack thought it, he still didn't believe what he'd seen was innocent. He couldn't shake the feeling that his father had hired the man for some kind of job that involved whoever lived in that brownstone across the street.

He glanced at the time. Earlier, when he'd decided to stop by the cemetery, he knew he'd be cutting it close to meet his appointment back at the ranch. He prided himself on his punctuality. But if he kept sitting here, he would miss his meeting.

Jack reached for his cell phone. The least he could do was call and reschedule. But before he could key in the number, the door of the brownstone opened and a young woman with long blond hair came out.

As she started down the street in the opposite direction, Ed got out of his car. Jack watched him make a quick call on his cell phone as he began to follow the woman.

CHAPTER TWO

THE BLONDE HAD the look of a rich girl, from her long coiffed hair to her stylish short skirt and crisp white top to the pale blue sweater lazily draped over one arm. Hypnotized by the sexy swish of her skirt, Jack couldn't miss the glint of silver jewelry at her slim wrist or the name-brand bag she carried.

Jack grabbed the gun he kept in his glove box and climbed out of his truck. The blonde took a quick call on her cell phone as she walked. She quickened her steps, pocketing her phone. Was she meeting someone and running late? A date?

As she turned down another narrow street, he saw Ed on the opposite side of the street on his phone again. Telling someone...what?

He felt his anxiety rise as Ed ended his call and put away his phone as he crossed the street. Jack took off after the two. He tucked the gun into the waist of his jeans. He had no idea what was going on, but all his instincts told him the blonde, whoever she was, was in danger.

As he reached the corner, he saw that Ed was now only yards behind the woman, his limp even more pronounced. The narrow alley-like street was empty of people and businesses. The neighborhood rejuvenation hadn't reached this street yet. There was dirt and debris along the front of the vacant buildings. So where was the woman going?

Jack could hear the blonde's heels making a *tap, tap, tap* sound as she hurried along. Ed's work boots made no sound as he gained on the woman.

As Ed increased his steps, he pulled out what looked like a white cloth from a plastic bag in his pocket. Discarding the bag, he suddenly rushed down the deserted street toward the woman.

Jack raced after him. Ed had reached the woman, looping one big strong arm around her from behind and lifting her off her feet. Her blue sweater fell to the ground along with her purse as she struggled.

Ed was fighting to get the cloth over her mouth and nose. The blonde was frantically moving her head back and forth and kicking her legs and arms wildly. Some of her kicks were connecting. Ed let out several cries of pain as well as a litany of curses as she managed to knock the cloth from his hand.

After setting her feet on the ground, Ed grabbed a handful of her hair and jerked her head back. Cocking his other fist, he reared back as if to slug her.

Running up, Jack pulled the gun, and hit the man with the stock of his handgun.

Ed released his hold on the woman's hair, stumbled

and fell to his knees as she staggered back from him, clearly shaken. Her gaze met his as Jack heard a vehicle roaring toward them from another street. Unless he missed his guess, it was cohorts of Ed's.

As a van came careening around the corner, Jack cried "Come on!" to the blonde. She stood a few feet away looking too stunned and confused to move. He quickly stepped to her, grabbed her hand and, giving her only enough time to pick up her purse from the ground, pulled her down the narrow alley.

Behind them, the van came to a screeching stop. Jack looked back to see two men in the front of the vehicle. One jumped out to help Ed, who was holding the blonde's sweater to his bleeding head.

Jack tugged on her arm and she began to run with him again. They rounded a corner, then another one. He thought he heard the sound of the van's engine a block over and wanted to keep running, but he could tell she wasn't up to it. He dragged her into an inset open doorway to let her catch her breath.

They were both breathing hard. He could see that she was still scared, but the shock seemed to be wearing off. She eyed him as if having second thoughts about letting a complete stranger lead her down this dark alley.

"I'm not going to hurt you," he said. "I'm trying to protect you from those men who tried to abduct you."

She nodded, but didn't look entirely convinced. "Who are you?"

"Jack. My name is Jack Durand. I saw that man

following you," he said. "I didn't think, I just ran up behind him and hit him." It was close enough to the truth. "Who are *you?*"

"Cassidy Hamilton." No Texas accent. Nor did the name ring any bells. So what had they wanted with this young woman?

"Any idea who those guys were or why they were after you?"

She looked away, swallowed, then shook her head. "Do you think they're gone?"

"I don't think so." After he'd seen that wad of money his father had given Ed, he didn't think the men would be giving up. "I suspect they are now looking for both of us." When he'd looked back earlier, he'd thought Ed or one of the other men had seen him. He'd spent enough time at his father's warehouse that most of the dockworkers knew who he was.

But why would his father want this woman abducted? It made no sense and yet it was the only logical conclusion he could draw given what he'd witnessed at the cemetery.

"Let's wait a little bit. Do you live around here?"

"I was staying with a friend."

"I don't think you should go back there. That man has been following you for several blocks."

She nodded and hugged herself, looking scared. He figured a lot of what had almost happened hadn't yet registered. Either that or what had almost happened didn't come as a complete surprise to her. Which made him even more curious why his father would want to abduct this woman.

ED URDAHL COULDN'T believe his luck. He'd picked a street that he knew wouldn't have anyone on it this time of the day. On top of that, the girl had been in her own little world. She hadn't been paying any attention to him as he'd moved up directly behind her.

The plan had been simple. Grab her, toss her into the van that would come speeding up at the perfect time and make a clean, quick getaway so no one would be the wiser.

It should have gone down without any trouble.

He'd been so intent on the woman in front of him, though, that he hadn't heard the man come up behind him until it was too late. Even if someone had intervened, Ed had been pretty sure he could handle it. He'd been a wrestler and boxer growing up. Few men were stupid enough to take him on.

The last thing he'd expected was to be smacked in the back of the head by some do-gooder. What had he been hit with, anyway? Something hard and cold. A gun? The blow had knocked him senseless and the next thing he'd known he was on the sidewalk bleeding. As he'd heard the van engine roaring in his direction, he'd fought to keep from blacking out as whoever had blindsided him had gotten away with the blonde.

"What happened?" his brother Alec demanded now. Ed leaned against the van wall in the back, his head hurting like hell. "I thought you had it all worked out."

"How the hell do I know?" He was still bleeding like a stuck pig. "Just get out of here. *Drive!*" he yelled at the driver, Nick, a dockworker he'd used before for less-than-legal jobs. "Circle the block until I can think of what to do."

Ed caught a whiff of the blonde's perfume and realized he was holding her sweater to his bleeding skull. He took another sniff of it. *Nice.* He tried to remember exactly what had transpired. It had all happened so fast. "Did you see who hit me?" he asked.

"I saw a man and a woman going down the alley," Alec said. "I thought you said she'd be alone?"

That's what he had thought. It had all been set up in a way that should have gone off like clockwork. So where had whoever hit him come from? "So neither of you got a look at the guy?"

Nick cleared his throat. "I thought at first that he was working *with* you."

"Why would you think that?" Ed demanded, his head hurting too much to put up with such stupid remarks. "The son of a bitch coldcocked me with something."

"A gun. It was a gun," Alec said. "I saw the light catch on the metal when he tucked it back into his pants."

"He was carrying a gun?" Ed sat up, his gaze going to Nick. "Is that why you thought he was part of the plan?"

"No, I didn't see the gun," Nick said. "I just assumed he was in on it because of who he was."

Ed pressed the sweet-smelling sweater to his head and tried not to erupt. "Are you going to make me guess? Or are you frigging going to tell me who was he?"

"Jack Durand."

"What?" Ed couldn't believe his ears. What were the chances that Tom Durand's son would show up on this particular street? Unless his father had sent him? That made no sense. *Why pay me if he sent his son?*

"You're sure it was Jack?"

"Swear on my mother's grave," Nick said as he drove in wider circles. "I saw him clear as a bell. He turned in the alley to look back. It was Jack, all right."

"Go back to that alley," Ed ordered. Was this Tom's backup plan in case Ed failed? Or was this all part of Tom's real plan? Either way, it appeared Jack Durand had the girl.

CASSIDY LOOKED AS if she might make a run for it at any moment. That would be a huge mistake on her part. But Jack could tell that she was now pretty sure she shouldn't be trusting him. He wasn't sure how much longer he could keep her here. She reached for her phone, but he laid a hand on her arm.

"That's the van coming back," he said quietly. At the sound of the engine growing nearer, he signaled her not to make a sound as he pulled her deeper into the darkness of the doorway recess. The van drove slowly up the alley. He'd feared they would come back. That's why he'd been hesitant to move from their hiding place.

Jack held his breath as he watched the blonde, afraid she might do something crazy like decide to take her chances and run. He wouldn't have blamed her. For all she knew, he could have been in on the abduction and was holding her here until the men in the van came back for her.

The driver of the van braked next to the open doorway. The engine sat idling. Jack waited for the sound of a door opening. He'd put the gun into the back waistband of his jeans before he'd grabbed the blonde, thinking the gun might frighten her. As much as he wanted to pull it now, he talked himself out of it.

At least for the moment. He didn't want to get involved in any gunplay—especially with the young woman here. He'd started carrying the gun when he'd worked for his father and had to take the day's proceeds to a bank drop late at night. It was a habit he'd gotten used to even after he'd quit. Probably because of the type of people who worked with his father.

After what seemed like an interminable length of time, the van driver pulled away.

Jack let out the breath he'd been holding. "Come on. I'll see that you get someplace safe where you can call the police," he said and held out his hand.

She hesitated before she took it. They moved through the dark shadows of the alley to the next street. The sky above them had turned a deep silver in the evening light. It was still hot, little air in the tight, narrow street.

He realized that wherever Cassidy Hamilton had been headed, she hadn't planned to return until much later—thus the sweater. He wanted to question her, but now wasn't the time.

At the edge of the buildings, Jack peered down the street. He didn't see the van or Ed's green car. But he also didn't think they had gone far. Wouldn't they expect her to call the police? The area would soon be crawling with cop cars. So what would Ed do?

A few blocks from the deserted area where they'd met, they reached a more commercial section. The street was growing busier as people got off work. Restaurants began opening for the evening meal as boutiques and shops closed. Jack spotted a small bar with just enough patrons that he thought they could blend in.

"Let's go in here," he said. "I don't know about you, but I could use a drink. You should be able to make a call from here. Once I know you're safe…"

They took a table at the back away from the television over the bar. He removed his Stetson and put it on the seat next to him. When Cassidy wasn't looking, he removed the .45 from the waistband of his jeans and slid it under the hat.

"What do you want to drink?" he asked as the waitress approached.

"White wine," she said and plucked nervously at the torn corner of her blouse. Other than the torn blouse, she looked fine physically. But emotionally, he wasn't sure how much of a toll this would take on her over the long haul. That was if Ed didn't find her.

"I'll have whiskey," he said, waving the waitress off. He had no idea what he was going to do now. He told himself he just needed a jolt of alcohol. He'd been playing this by ear since seeing his father and Ed at the cemetery.

Now he debated what he was going to do with this woman given the little he knew. The last thing he wanted, though, was to get involved with the police. He was sure Ed and his men had seen him, probably recognized him. Once his father found out that it had been his son who'd saved the blonde…

The waitress put two drinks in front of them and left. He watched the blonde take a sip. She'd said her name was Cassidy Hamilton. She'd also said she didn't know why anyone would want to abduct her off the street, but he suspected that wasn't true.

"So is your old man rich or something?" he asked and took a gulp of the whiskey.

She took a sip of her wine as if stalling, her gaze lowered. He got his first really good look at her. She was a knockout. When she lifted her eyes finally, he thought he might drown in all that blue.

"I only ask because I'm trying to understand why those men were after you." She could be a famous model or even an actress. He didn't follow pop culture, hardly ever watched television and hadn't been to the movies in ages. All he knew was, at the very least, she'd grown up with money. "If you're famous or something, I apologize for not knowing."

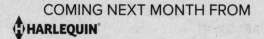

Natalie's car suddenly swerved. Tension snapped through
Clint. She barreled off the road and into the lot of a
supermarket, crashing broadside into a parked car.

His pulse hammering, Clint made the turn and skidded
to a stop next to her car. He jumped out and rushed to her.
Thank God no one was in the other vehicle. Natalie sat
upright behind the steering wheel. The deflated air bag
sagged in front of her. The injuries she may have sustained
from the air bag deploying ticked off in his brain.

He tried to open the door but it was locked. He banged
on the window. "Natalie! Are you all right?"

She turned and stared up at him. Her face was flushed
red, abrasions already darkening on her skin. His heart
rammed mercilessly against his sternum as she slowly hit
the unlock button. He yanked the door open and crouched
down to get a closer look at her.

"Are you hurt?" he demanded.

HIEXP0816

"I'm not sure." She took a deep breath as if she'd only just remembered to breathe. "I don't understand what happened. I was driving along and the air bag suddenly burst from the steering wheel." She reached for the wheel and then drew back, uncertain what to do with her hands. "I don't understand," she repeated.

"I'm calling for help." Clint made the call to 9-1-1 and then he called his friend Lieutenant Chet Harper. Every instinct cautioned Clint that Natalie was wrong about not being able to trust herself.

There was someone else—someone very close to her—she shouldn't trust. He intended to keep her safe until he identified that threat.

Don't miss DARK WHISPERS
by USA TODAY *bestselling author Debra Webb,*
available in September 2016 wherever
Harlequin® Intrigue books and ebooks are sold.

www.Harlequin.com

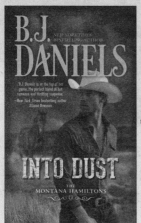

THE WORLD IS BETTER WITH

Romance

Harlequin has everything from contemporary, passionate and heartwarming to suspenseful and inspirational stories.

Whatever your mood, we have a romance just for you!

Connect with us to find your next great read, special offers and more.

f /HarlequinBooks

🐦 @HarlequinBooks

www.HarlequinBlog.com

www.Harlequin.com/Newsletters

⊞ HARLEQUIN®

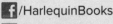

A *Romance* FOR EVERY MOOD™

www.Harlequin.com